Missing Persons

Paradise Cruises Series: Book 3

AE Moran

The Invisible Publishing Company

Contents

Chapter 1: Jenn

"Oh, my God!" I gush. "Look at that view!"

"It's just the ocean," my boyfriend Donovan tells me. "You're going to be seeing a lot of that on this cruise. Come on. We have to check in and find our cabin before the safety briefing starts."

"We already checked in and the staff already took our luggage up to the cabin. I want to stay down here. We can go up to the cabin later." I pace down the windows of the cruise ship's main piazza.

It opens onto the grand concourse. I get distracted from the piazza windows to stare in at the tons of stores, restaurants, theaters, casinos, night clubs, and even laser tag venues.

"This ship has everything!" I exclaim.

Donovan comes over and takes my hand. "I can see I'm going to have to keep an eye on you. Don't wander off. The briefing will start from the piazza. We should stay here if we aren't going to go check out our cabin."

"We still have a few minutes." I take a step into the concourse. "We could spend the rest of our lives here and never get tired of it."

"I'm sure we would find some reason to go home. We would run out of money if you got stuck in the casino for too long."

I laugh, but then we notice people gathering on the piazza. We join them and smile at other couples while we wait for the safety briefing to start.

Allie, the ship's activity coordinator, takes her place at the other end of the piazza to welcome us all on board the Paradise Cruise ship *Electric Emerald*.

I don't hear anything else. I can't stop staring at the man standing next to her.

He's a big guy with powerful, muscular shoulders, a veiny neck, and strong hands he keeps clasped in front of him.

He has sandy hair and flashing, steely eyes that flick through the crowd with a sharp, penetrating gaze.

He wears a stunning coal grey suit tailored perfectly to his chiseled physique. I get so distracted by the guy that I barely notice when Allie leads the crowd to one side to show them around the pools and the other activity areas on the deck.

Donovan definitely notices me gaping at the man. "What are you doing?" Donovan hisses in my face. "Are you trying to make me mad?"

I try to tear my gaze away from the guy, but it's kind of hard when he keeps standing there right in front of us.

"Quit staring!" Donovan whispers.

I mumble, "Sorry," and turn away again, but it doesn't work.

I actually stumble the next time we have to walk anywhere. Donovan has to pull me by the hand to get my attention.

He takes advantage of the crowd's movements to steer me to one side where he can get in my face without interrupting the briefing.

"What is the matter with you?!" he demands in a harsh undertone. "We're supposed to be taking a romantic cruise together so we can get serious about each other and you're out here drooling over another guy! Now we're missing the briefing! I can't believe you!"

"I'm not drooling over him!" I explain. "He looks exactly like my cousin, Flynn. He vanished overseas years ago. No one has seen or heard from him since. This could be him."

"Will you knock it off?! Do you really expect me to accept a pathetic lie like that?"

"It isn't a lie, Donovan! It's the truth! I can prove it to you. You can ask my parents...."

"I'm not going to ask your parents! Stop looking at the guy! Are you here with me or not?"

"Yes, of course, I am! I wouldn't look at another guy...."

"You just were! Don't do it again or we're going to have a massive problem."

He takes my hand and storms back to the briefing, but the same problem keeps happening. That same guy is always there at the front of the crowd—right in front of my eyes.

I spend the rest of the safety tour staring at the floor, but it's too late. I've already seen the guy.

Could he be my cousin? Did he lose his memory or something—or has he been hiding from our family for some reason?

The tour finally ends. Donovan and I go up to our cabin where I don't have to see the guy, but all these questions keep spinning around in my head.

I go out to the balcony and look out over the ocean. Donovan is right. I'm going to be seeing a lot of it on this cruise, but it calms me. It would take my mind off my problems, but it doesn't take my mind off this.

I just hope I don't see the guy too much on the cruise. Maybe our paths won't cross again and I can stop thinking about him.

I go back inside and find Donovan sitting on the couch reading the activities program. "What do you want to do tonight?" he asks.

"You're right about this ship having everything. We could go to a show, go to the casino, play pool...."

I sit down next to him on the couch and pull his arm around me. It looks like he's ready to drop the subject and move on. Thank goodness.

I smile up at him. "We could always stay in."

She smirks and his cheeks turn bright red. "We could."

"We could never leave this cabin until the ship comes back to port. We're supposed to be getting romantic, aren't we?"

"Romantic—yes. We aren't supposed to get ourselves hospitalized."

I laugh. "We would get room service. We wouldn't go hungry."

"I'm talking about the other thing." He leans in and kisses me before he leans back and strokes my cheek. "I love you. I want us to have a big, beautiful future together—so we would need to go out sometimes."

"Okay. So what do *you* want to do tonight?"

He picks up the program. "None of the musical acts appeal to me—and I'm not into seeing anything musical theater."

"Neither am I—but they do have movies."

"I'm not interested in anything they're showing, either."

"What about the comedy club? Neither of us gambles, so that's out."

"Let's have dinner at a restaurant first. Maybe inspiration will strike when we get down to the concourse."

I get a very brief flash of doubt. What if I see that guy down on the concourse? What if he's eating dinner in the same restaurant?

I shake those thoughts out of my head. I'm sure I can avoid the guy. I'm sure I can even avoid looking at the guy. We can always go to another restaurant if he's there.

I pick up the program again. "Now the question becomes what to eat and where to eat it."

We launch into a discussion to decide where to go for dinner, but the same questions keep coming back to haunt me. How can I stop thinking about the guy if I don't find out for certain if he is my cousin?

Chapter 2: Marco

My girlfriend Angeline leans over the railing of the *Electric Emerald*. She breathes a sigh when she looks down at the waterline. "This is so magical! I can't believe this is actually happening."

I ease in behind her and slip my arms around her waist to hold her from behind. "It's going to be perfect." I kiss the side of her head. "This is going to be the perfect start to the rest of our lives together."

She turns around in my grasp and slips her arms around my neck to kiss me straight on. "Were you serious when you said you wanted us to get married?"

"Of course. I wouldn't have said it if I didn't mean it." I arch my eyebrow at her. "Is that what you want?"

"Of course," she exclaims. "I just didn't know you felt that way. You're always so cryptic about it."

"I wasn't trying to be cryptic. I just wanted to be sure before I said anything."

"Why weren't you sure? We've been dating for over a year. You introduced me to your family and everything. If that isn't serious, I don't know what is."

"That was just a test run. I wanted to see how you got along with everyone."

"So how did I do?"

"You were great. They love you. They think you're the one."

Her eyes lock on me. "Am I the one?"

"I think so. I wouldn't have said I wanted to get married if I wasn't sure."

She kisses me again. "So is that why you brought me on this cruise—so you could propose to me under the moonlight."

I feel my cheeks burn. I have to look away. "I might have."

She laughs, pulls away, and takes my hand. "Let's go check out the concourse before the safety briefing. I want to look at all the....."

She breaks off when a bunch of other passengers assemble on the piazza for the safety briefing and tour. Allie, the activities coordinator, shows up and introduces Troy Nixon, the head of security.

He's a big guy who stands there like a wall of granite through the whole briefing. He never takes his eyes off the passengers. I can just see him evaluating all of us to decide which of us is going to become his problem in the future.

I glance down to smile at Angeline—and I stop dead in my tracks when I see another woman across the room. She stands facing the front of the tour group—and then she turns her head to look at the man next to her.

They hold a brief, whispered conversation. I see her face from the front in that moment before she turns side on.

The tour group migrates toward the pools, but I don't move. I can't. My gaze rivets on that woman. She has long, dark hair and delicate features. She's almost as tall as I am with a curvy, succulent figure.

Her tight pink pencil skirt shows off nicely rounded hips and thighs. She wears a tight, bright pink tank top that reveals a faint hint of a lacy black bra underneath.

Angeline snaps me out of my trance by elbowing me hard in the ribs. I look over to find her glaring at me.

I try to pay attention to the tour, but my gaze keeps migrating back to that woman. She keeps talking to that man standing next to her and then he takes her off to one side so they can have a private conversation.

It doesn't look like a nice conversation. They look like they're arguing and the boat hasn't even left the dock yet.

It looks like I'm heading in the same direction considering the way Angeline is giving me another death glare. I drag my attention away from the woman, but the tour is already ending.

She starts in on me the minute the tour breaks up. At least we're standing outside in the breezeway. People can still hear us, but it isn't as bad as if she did in the piazza or the concourse.

"Is this really the way you plan to conduct our whole hypothetical marriage—staring at other women?" she snaps. "You said you wanted us to come on this cruise so you could propose to me. Was that just some kind of game?"

"Of course not! I wasn't staring at her...."

"Are you trying to gaslight me or something? I saw you with my own eyes! I'm surprised her husband or boyfriend or whatever he is didn't come over and punch your lights out! It was creepy!"

"You don't understand!" I tell her. "It's just that..."

"I understand you were staring at another woman. What more is there to understand?"

"She looks exactly like my sister, okay? That's why I was staring at her! I was taken by surprise. I wasn't staring at her because I was interested in her or attracted to her or anything like that!"

She snorts at me. "Now I know you're playing me. You don't have a sister!"

"Not anymore! Will you just listen to me for two seconds? My sister Becca got lost when she was six years old. She fell overboard on a fishing boat when we were on vacation. They never found her body and everyone in my family thinks there's a chance she could have survived. My parents spent a fortune trying to find her—okay? I was staring at that woman because she looks exactly like her. It could be her! You never found out about it because it never came up! I just introduced you to my family. It's an old story and everyone wants to forget it ever happened because they think they'll never find her. It isn't like we haven't always had other things to talk about. It just never came up."

"How would you know what she looks like if she disappeared when she was six years old? That woman is almost thirty!"

"My parents had computer-generated renderings done of what Becca would look like now. They keep running the renderings through Police and government databases trying to find someone who looks like her—because it could be her! Come on! I have to find out. This has been haunting my family for almost twenty-five years!"

She narrows her eyes and purses her lips. "You better not be lying about this."

"Why don't you call my parents and ask them? They'll tell you it's true. They'll be out of their minds when they find out we found someone who looks like Becca."

She won't stop glaring at me. "You're on this cruise so you can pay attention to me—not so you can hobnob with other women."

"I'm not hobnobbing with anyone, sweetheart. Give me a break."

"Just leave it alone, okay?" she snaps. "You didn't have to stare at her like that. You could have waited and approached her later—after you explained it to me."

"I'm sorry. I was just surprised and shocked. I didn't mean to offend you." I make a snap decision. "I won't look at her again. I promise."

"You better not," she snarls.

I slip my hand into hers. "Can we go back to acting romantic now?"

She looks away. "I'll think about it."

"Let's go over to the concourse." I lean and kiss her on the cheek. "They have jewelry stores there."

She turns around, but only to glare at me again. "I won't marry you if this is the kind of stuff we have to go through."

"It was a simple miscommunication. It could have happened to anyone. Come on. Let's put it behind us and concentrate on us. Finding out about her won't affect us anyway—whether she is Becca or not."

She follows me when I lead her to the concourse, but she stays quiet even when we do pass jewelry stores.

I take her into one of the restaurants to get lunch, but I can't help seeing that woman pass the window.

At least she passes behind Angeline's back. Angeline doesn't see the woman nor does Angeline see me looking at her.

Who is she? Is she Becca all grown up?

She looks exactly like the renderings. The service that generated them gave us five different possibilities for what Becca would look like now.

They all look different, but they're similar enough to this woman. It has to be her—if Becca is even still alive.

I have to find out. I can't get off this ship until I know for certain.

Chapter 3: Jenn

Donovan squeezes my hand, leans in close, and shoots his eyes past me toward the other side of the concourse. "There's a jewelry store over there."

"Do you need another gold chain or something?"

He bursts into a grin and his cheeks flush. "I was thinking of getting something for you."

"Don't let me stop you."

He laughs and we continue down the concourse to one of the casinos. "Do you ever wonder what the big deal is all about?"

"I suppose we could turn it into an anthropological expedition—like studying the aliens in their native habitat."

"Yeah! Let's do it!" he exclaims. "Then we can say we did it and we never have to do it again."

"Okay. Let's go."

We walk into the casino. He kisses me on the cheek. "I'll go get us some drinks. You wander around and see if you can understand their language."

Now it's my turn to laugh. He goes to the bar. I meander around, watch the tables, and stop at one of them. A guy is standing there holding a bunch of chips, but he isn't playing.

He looks like he's observing the aliens in their native habitat, too. The chips don't really make him look like he belongs here.

He wears his dark, chestnut hair buzzed high on the side with a tightly gelled cap of curls on top. His hazel-green eyes glitter when he turns to me.

He has chiseled features and a very square jawline. He could be a supermodel, but he has a laid-back, easy-going, let-it-ride kind of vibe.

He looks at me way too closely, transfers his chips to his left hand, and sticks out his right. "I'm Marco de Rossi. What's your name? Where are you from?"

I look down at him. "My name is Taken. I'm here with someone. Thanks but no thanks."

"I wasn't hitting on you," he tells me. "I'm just asking."

I spot Donovan coming with our drinks, so I walk away and meet up with him. "The aliens at that table are on the prowl for Earth women," I tell him. "I think we better make it back to the *Enterprise.*"

He snorts with laughter. "Let's try the blackjack table. They might be friendlier there."

We turn to go check out the blackjack table, but right then, I see the guy from the safety briefing—the one who looks like my cousin Flynn.

I try not to react, but I wind up gasping in spite of myself. It's too late. Donovan sees the guy, too.

He's wearing a dark, navy blue suit tonight with a matching tie, gold tie pin, and a bright red pocket square. Every speck of his shirt and sleeve cuffs are blindingly, immaculate white. Rarely have I seen a guy who dresses this well.

He keeps his hair perfectly combed and he has a manicure. He looks fantastic.

He crosses my line of sight, walks up to the bar, and stands there talking to the bartender while she serves him a drink. He towers over every other man in the room—or maybe it's just his presence that makes it seem that way.

He turns halfway around so I can see his face. He scans the casino, but he doesn't notice me standing there with my eyes hanging out of their sockets.

Donovan definitely notices and glares at me. I turn away, he takes my hand, and I follow him across the room to the blackjack table, but he doesn't let it go.

I stand there with my back to the bar, but the temperature in the room definitely drops a few dozen degrees.

He leans across and whispers in my ear. "We're going to have an issue with this when we get out of here."

I cringe. What am I supposed to do—not notice that this guy looks exactly like my cousin? It isn't like I'm running him down proposing marriage or anything.

I try to pretend that the other guy isn't right here in the same casino with me and Donovan. The guy could have walked out already. I could be going crazy for no reason.

Donovan steps up to the table and plays a few rounds of blackjack. He wins some and loses some. He doesn't take to it very well—probably because he's never gambled before.

He comes back over to me after half an hour. "Do you want to play?"

"Naw," I tell him. "Let's get out of here. I think we've seen enough of the aliens for now."

He nods. "I'm gonna go to the bathroom. I'll meet you back over here and then we'll head out."

He kisses me on the cheek, but I would have to be in a coma not to feel the resentment.

He walks away. I watch the next game since I have nothing better to do.

Someone startles me out of my skin by saying my name. "Jenn Hayworth?"

I spin around and my world drops out from under my feet when I come face to face with the guy in the suit—the guy who looks exactly like my missing cousin.

I can't make a sound. He can't be standing right here in front of me. Did he recognize me? Does he remember me? Is he coming to talk to me so I can help him get back in touch with the family?

"I need to ask you some questions," he tells me. "I hope you don't mind. Is now a bad time?"

"I.......Are you.....Do you know me?" I blurt out. "Do you recognize me? Have we met somewhere before? I swear I know you from somewhere. Where are you from? Does your family live in Wichita Falls? Have you ever been there?"

Now his eyes fall out of their sockets. "Excuse me?"

"I was just asking because....I just wondered...."

His expression clears. "Look. I'm flattered that you're interested, but I'm happily married and I'm not interested in anyone else. I only ask because I need to know a few details about your itinerary—where along our route you'll be disembarking and whether you have visas for all the countries we'll be stopping in."

"I.....what?" I stammer. "Why do you want to know that?"

"I'm the Chief of Security for the *Electric Emerald.* Didn't you know that? I saw you at the safety briefing. Allie introduced me to all of you. I know you saw me there because I saw you. I just need to clarify all the passenger itineraries. It's part of my job. I didn't come over here to hit on you or for you to hit on me—and no, I have never been to Wichita Falls. I would definitely remember that—and no, I don't know you or recognize you."

I cover my eyes. "Oh, my God! I can't believe it."

"Don't worry about it," he tells me. "We can forget it."

"I'm really sorry." I stick out my hand. "I wasn't paying attention to the briefing because you look exactly like my cousin who went missing five years ago. I wasn't sure if you were him. I'm sorry. I didn't catch your name before—and I wasn't trying to hit on you. I was just trying to find out if you were him—or if you lost your memory—or something like that."

"Oh, I see." He shakes my hand. "Well.....I never went missing. I've been working here longer than five years. People would have noticed if I went missing."

"Okay." I smile at him. "Thank you—for clearing that up. I was going crazy wondering who you were."

"It's all right. I'm glad I could put the mystery to rest. Can you tell me now if you have all your visas?"

"Yes!" I scramble for my purse. "I have my passport here."

He pulls out his phone and snaps pictures of my visas. "Your booking with the cruise line states that you're sharing a cabin with Donavan McNulty. Is that correct?"

"Yes! He's my boyfriend. He's here somewhere. He should be coming back soon."

"Just tell him to bring his passport by my office—or he can show it to me if he sees me walking around the ship."

"Okay." I smile at him again. "Thanks. I guess I'll see you around."

He nods. "I'm sure of it."

He's just about to walk away when Donovan comes back. Neither Troy nor I see Donovan coming before he barges up to us, grabs me, and shoves his arm between me and Troy.

Donovan yanks me away and pushes Troy away from me at the same time. "Back off, pal," Donovan snaps. "Watch your step the next time you start hitting on another man's woman."

I start to say, "Donovan....."

"I wasn't hitting on her, Mr. McNulty," Troy begins.

Donovan freezes. "How do you know my name?"

I try to break out of his hold. "Donovan....you don't understand ....."

"I understand perfectly. Come on. We're leaving."

He clamps his hand around my elbow and marches me out of the casino. I keep saying, "Donovan—hey! Will you listen to me?! It wasn't what you think!"

"I saw perfectly well what it was and it was exactly what I think," he snaps over his shoulder. "I told you we would have an issue with this and now we do."

He stops at the elevator, stabs his finger into the button, and finally lets go of my arm. My elbow hurts where he held onto me too tightly. Should I be worried that he hurt me when he lost his temper?

"He was not hitting on me—and I was not hitting on him, Donovan!" I tell him. "He was asking me about...."

"Do you think I'm blind or something?! I saw you smiling at him. I'm a man. I saw perfectly well the way he was looking at you."

"He's married, Donovan! He wasn't hitting on me! He asked me about our itinerary stops and he told me to tell you...."

"You better not have told him anything." He steps into the elevator and lets me come in there by myself this time without trying to break my arm. "You should know better than to give out your personal details to strangers."

"He's the Chief of Security for the cruise ship, Donovan! It's his job to find out if we have visas for all our points of disembarkation!

He checked my passport and he told me to tell you to take yours to his office so he can check it! Will you pull your head out of the clouds? He's a married man and he was only talking to me because it's his job!"

"That doesn't stop you from dogging after him with your tongue hanging out, does it? You can't stop staring at the guy. What am I supposed to think?"

"I thought he was my cousin, okay?"

The elevator gets to our floor. We step out of the elevator and he turns around to point in my face. "Don't ever let me catch you talking to that guy again—or anyone else on this ship."

"I might have to talk to him! Don't you get that? He's in charge of security—and I'm not going to lock myself away and not talk to anyone else on the cruise, either. You have no reason to suspect me of anything with Troy...."

"Oh, so now you're on a first-name basis with him, is that it?" He storms through the door into our cabin. "I really thought we had something serious, but I can see I was mistaken. I can't trust you to go around flirting with every man who happens to pass you by."

"I WAS NOT FLIRTING WITH HIM!!" I fire back. "I talked to him once—and that was in a professional capacity."

"You were not smiling at him in a professional capacity! I know the way you smile at guys when you find them attractive...."

"He is attractive! That doesn't mean I was smiling at him like that! I was smiling because he cleared up my questions about him possibly being my cousin! Is it asking too much that I at least found out he isn't my cousin?"

"Yes, it's asking too much. I saw the way you were looking at him. You can't tell me you weren't interested."

"I *was* interested!" I roar. "I was interested in finding out who he was and whether he was my cousin! Okay? You can't possibly find any fault with that."

"I can find plenty of fault with the way you were looking at him, smiling at him, and blushing at him."

I throw up my hands. "I don't believe this. I can't believe you're making such a big deal about this."

"You don't think it's a big deal that I caught you making eyes at another man?!"

"I was not making eyes at him and it isn't like I've ever done this before! I was interested to find out if he was my cousin! That is the only reason I was interested in him and I'm not interested in him at all now that I know he isn't! Why can't you just believe me? It isn't like I've ever violated your trust before!"

"There's a first time for everything." He points past me. "You sleep in that bedroom over there. I don't want to be anywhere near you tonight."

He grabs his suitcase from its place by the couch, wheels it into the other bedroom, and slams the door in my face.

I sink onto the couch and cover my face with my hands. It's the first night of the cruise. How did this all go so wrong so fast?

Chapter 4: Marco

"I told you to stay away from her!" Angeline snaps. "I just saw you in there hitting on her!"

"I wasn't hitting on her! I was trying to talk to her—to find out who she is!"

"I saw you, Marco!" she fumes. "I saw you staring at her! You can't tell me that was a totally innocent, 'Hi, how are you?'"

"Yes, it was! I tried to introduce myself and she shut me down! She blurted out that she's taken and here with someone else—which I already knew!"

"So she thought you were hitting on her, too!" Angeline fires back. "I knew it!"

"I was not hitting on her, baby! How am I supposed to find out if she's my sister if I don't talk to her?!"

"Don't give me that sister crap again! How stupid do you think I am?!"

"I don't think you're stupid, but I have to find out about this! I don't see why you can't be more understanding! You can't expect me to walk away from this! I would never be able to live with myself!"

"Fine. You go talk to her and leave me the hell alone. You go talk to her and then go home alone. I never should have come on this cruise with you."

She starts to walk away toward the elevators. I go after her. "Aw, come on! Don't be like that! It was totally innocent! I swear it! Why don't you contact my parents and ask them about Becca?"

She rounds on me spitting tacks. "I'm not going to contact your parents, Marco! This isn't about your stupid sister if you even ever had one! I saw the way you were talking to her! You can't tell me there wasn't something going on between you!"

"How can there be anything between us when I don't even know her?! I don't even know her name. She wouldn't even tell me."

She snorts at me and gets into the elevator. She doesn't stop me from getting in there with her. "Come on, baby," I tell her. "I need you to support me on this. This is important to me and my whole family. We can't be together if you're gonna fly off the handle about stuff like this."

She won't look at me. "We aren't going to be together if I can't trust you."

"Then trust me on this. I could talk to her and find out that she is my sister and then you would know there's nothing between us. Why can't you stand by me on this?"

"Because you could just as easily find out that she isn't your sister and then there *would* be something between you! Don't go making it out like I'm crazy or something and seeing something that isn't there!"

"I have never given you any reason not to trust me. I have never looked sideways at another woman and I never would. My interest in her is totally innocent."

"I don't believe you!" She storms out of the elevator, barges down the hall to our cabin, and blasts into it in a rage. I've never seen her like this before.

She stomps over to her suitcase, wheels it into the bedroom, slings it onto the bed, opens it, and starts taking out her pajamas and other bedtime stuff.

I go in there and start to sit down on the edge of the bed to talk some sense into her.

"Don't get comfortable," she snaps. "You're sleeping in the other room tonight."

I stare up at her in shock. She's throwing me out—over something like this? Seriously?

It takes me a minute to fully believe that she actually means it. She goes into the bathroom and shuts and locks the door to change her clothes. She comes out in her pajamas.

I can't believe what I'm seeing. She has never pushed me away like this since we first started dating.

She completely ignores me and refuses to look at me while she puts her hair up, takes off her makeup, washes her face, and brushes her teeth.

I guess that's it, then. I stand up, walk out into the living room, and take hold of my suitcase handle to wheel it into the other bedroom.

I barely take two steps before she shuts the door to her room and locks that, too.

I snort to myself and go into my room to change and go to bed. If this is the way she wants it, then this is the way it's going to be.

I change my clothes and get into bed. I have to resist the urge to get on the internet and search the ship's passenger list to find out who that woman is.

I'm going to find out about her one way or the other. My relationship with Angeline isn't as important as the agony, heartache, and uncertainty my family has been going through for the last twenty-five years.

My parents had it the worst, but my brother and I went through it right along with them.

I remember the day Becca disappeared. We never say she died because we don't know. It would have been easier if she did die.

That was the day my family changed. We had a happy, loving, blissful family before that.

That day haunted all of us, especially my parents. They made it their mission to find her, dead or alive. They paid a team of forensic divers to go down into the river and search for Becca's body even after the Police called off the search.

Not even the Police declared her officially dead. They listed her as *Missing*. She's still listed as missing to this day.

The years only seemed to make my parents more determined—and more haunted. They loved me and my brother. They gave us everything we could ever want, but Becca's ghost kept haunting our family in the background—even in the good times.

No way would I ever let the sun go down on that. Angeline isn't the woman I thought she was if she can't support me on this.

I always thought she would be there for me through thick and thin. She even said she would be and I believed her.

That obviously isn't true. This is such a small incident compared to what it might be. We would face much bigger challenges than this if we got married. How can I trust her not to fly off the handle over something even bigger?

I didn't do anything wrong. That's what really stings. She's acting like I cheated on her or something. She has no reason to suspect me of anything. She might at least give me the benefit of the doubt—but no.

I don't know what I'm going to do about her, but I do know what I'm going to do about that woman.

I'm going to find her. I'm going to talk to her and I'm going to get some answers. I won't let anyone stop me.

Chapter 5: Jenn

I come out of my room showered, dressed, and ready for the day. I walk into the living room, sit down on the couch, and pick up the activities program just as Donovan comes out of the other bedroom.

He comes out showered, dressed, and ready for the day, too. "I'm going out for a while," he tells me.

I reply, "See you later," over my shoulder.

Good. He needs to take some time to cool off—since he clearly didn't do it last night.

There are a lot of activities on this list that I would like to do, but I make up my mind to stay in the cabin today. He can't possibly find any fault with anything I do if I don't see anyone.

How ironic that I came on a luxury romantic cruise. I'll probably wind up spending the rest of it locked in the cabin.

I throw the program on the table. Why am I even looking at it when I don't plan to do any of the activities?

I might go out tomorrow if Donovan calms down. Oh, what am I saying? If he doesn't calm down—if he keeps pulling this jealous boyfriend nonsense—I'll have to go out. I can't let him pressure me to stay inside all the time. That would be unacceptable.

I pick up the room service menu. I might as well eat breakfast.

I'll give him one day to come to his senses. Then we're going to have to have a serious conversation about this relationship.

I guess it's a good thing I'm finding out about him before we got serious with each other. He's showing his controlling and maybe even violent side.

I still have a bruise on my elbow from where he grabbed me last night.

I pick up my phone to call in the room service order when someone knocks on the cabin door. It better not be that guy from the casino last night. He better not have tracked me down to hit on me a second time.

I stand up and open the door. My jaw drops again when I find myself standing in front of Troy Nixon, the Security Chief. Five other burly security guards stand behind him.

"Good morning, Mrs. Hayworth," he greets me.

"Um.....good morning. Can I help you with something? Donovan isn't here, but I told him about the visas. You'll have to work it out with him for him to show them to you."

"I'm not here about that. I was wondering if you would mind if we search your cabin." He holds up his hand. "It's entirely voluntary. We won't do it if you say you don't want us to."

"Why do you want to? Do you suspect us of anything?"

"No, of course not. It was the people who stayed in this cabin on the last cruise. They're suspected of stealing a bunch of jewels from a store on the last shore stop of their cruise. The authorities are wondering if the couple hid the jewels here in this room. Would you mind? It will only take a minute."

"Uh....okay. I guess so." I stand aside and the security team floods the cabin.

I stay by the door to keep out of their path. They spread out through the suite, check under all the beds, stick their arms between the mattresses, and even lift the lid off the toilet reservoir tank.

One of the security guys crawls along the baseboards pressing and checking them and the walls near them. The team checks all the outlets, all the light switch plates, all the door handles, the walls, and even behind the big screen TV in the living room.

I don't know what to think, but they don't find anything. I'm just wondering if I should be worried about this when Troy comes over to me. "It doesn't look like the stolen goods are here. We'll let the authorities know. Thank you for letting us in."

"Sure. No problem."

He ushers all the guards out of the room before Troy turns back to me. "Tell Donovan there's no hurry on the visa thing as long as we get it done before your first shore stop."

I nod. "I'll tell him. Thank you for stopping by."

"We really appreciate your cooperation on this. It would have been a nightmare if you said no."

I can't help but grin. He turns to leave. He's a really great guy. I realize now why he's the head of security. Nothing ruffles him.

He's about to walk out of the room when Donovan barges in again. I see exactly what he's thinking when his eyes dart back and forth between me and Troy. "What the hell is going on here?!" he demands and rounds on Troy. "I told you to stay away from her, you bastard!"

"I'm the Chief of Security for the ship, Mr. McNulty," Troy replies in his calmest tone. "I'm here on an official matter....."

"Oh, I'm sure sleeping with all the women on board is an official matter to you...."

"It wasn't like that, Donovan," I interrupt. "Troy is here to search the cabin...."

"You let him in?!" Donovan blares. "How many times do I have to tell you not to do that?!" Donovan spins around and starts getting in Troy's face. "You better not have searched my room. That would be illegal since you didn't get my consent first."

"Actually, this whole cabin is registered to both of you," Troy replies. "So Ms. Hayworth has as much right to consent to a search as you do."

Donovan gives a sick laugh. "Oh, I see how it is. You two are all cozy with each other now, aren't you? This is just great."

"The people who rented this cabin before you are suspected in a jewelry theft at one of their points of disembarkation," Troy goes on. "Ms. Hayworth was kind enough to let us search this cabin....."

"Don't give me that shit, you cocksucker!" Donovan snaps. "Do you think I don't see you horning in on my patch? Do you think I'm blind?"

Troy says, "Mr. McNulty," and I say, "Donovan," at the same time, but Donovan chops his hand at Troy to silence him.

"Just get out of here, man," Donovan snaps. "You've done enough damage for one day. Go on. Get out."

Troy keeps his expression passive the whole time. He thanks me one more time and leaves.

Donovan slams the door. I can't even fly off the handle on him. I already know what he's going to say before he even says it.

"You can't even tell me this was about your stupid, made-up cousin," he fumes. "What the hell was he doing in the cabin alone with you? I can't even walk out the door without you pulling this crap behind my back."

I watch him pace the cabin. It's over between us. I don't have to say it because we both know it.

He doesn't trust me. He doesn't believe me. He doesn't listen to a word I say.

He hurt me last night and he doesn't even know it. He's too up his own ass even to ask.

I can't have a relationship with him. That's all there is to it. I don't know what I was thinking getting involved with him, but it's over now.

I know what I was thinking when I got involved with him. He didn't act this way before.

Was he just trying to behave himself so he could get together with me? He's sure letting his true colors show now.

He paces the room with his hands on his hips. "What else did you tell him?" he demands. "What other personal information of mine did you tell him?"

"I didn't tell him anything." My voice sounds dead calm—or maybe just dead. I don't feel anything about our relationship ending. "He didn't ask for any personal information. He already has that on our cruise bookings."

He snorts at me. "The security guys better not have gone through my suitcase."

They didn't. They didn't need to go through his suitcase because there's no way the previous passengers could have hidden their jewels in Donovan McNulty's suitcase.

When did he get so paranoid? I realize it doesn't matter if they went through his suitcase. He would find an excuse either way.

He doesn't even have to suspect me of anything. Maybe he's making it all up so he can dump me.

He comes striding back over to me. "You can't see him again. I don't care what the situation is, but you can't see him again. Is that clear?"

"He's the Chief of Security for the ship. I have to see him when I get on and off at our shore stops. He has to check all of us on and off the ship."

He shakes his head. "Then you won't be able to get off the boat—and don't let me catch you talking to any other guys."

"What about waiters, bellboys, and lifeguards? Am I allowed to talk to them? What about the room service guy? Should I talk to him on the phone when I place my order—since I won't be leaving the cabin for the rest of the cruise? Should I use one of those extendable grasping claws to pass him the tip so we don't stand too close to each other?"

He stares at me in stunned shock for a minute—like really can't believe that I would say something like that. Does he really, honestly think I would put up with him laying all these restrictions on my life?

He reacts exactly the way I expect, throws up his hands, and storms off to his room. "You know what? We're finished." I hear him unzipping his suitcase and putting things in it. "I'm getting another cabin. You stay here. You can screw as many guys as you like. I don't care. They can have you. I'm done. You can delete my number from your phone. You won't need it anymore."

I sit down on the couch. That didn't take as long as I thought it would. I thought he would take longer to come around to it.

He throws all his belongings into his suitcase, zips it up, and wheels it out of the room without saying another word to me. I don't try to stop him. I'm better off without a sulking child like that.

Chapter 6: Jenn

I wander out onto the rear deck of the ship directly above the propellor. It churns up a thick froth of white foam in the wake behind the boat.

I bend over and look down at the chaotic jumble of waves, swells, and spray. The sea air smells extra salty here.

I raise my face into the sunshine. I feel good. I'm still at loose ends after my breakup with Donovan, but I'm going to be okay. I know that now.

I also know that the breakup was the best thing for me. I don't know how long my relationship with him would have lasted, but it would have come to an end eventually. It was doomed from the start.

I turn around to look up at the bridge. I can see the officers moving around, looking through binoculars, and pointing out at the ocean.

I wish I could be a fly on the wall and watch and hear what they're saying. I'm sure it would get boring after a while.

Piloting this ship can't be that different from driving a car on a long road trip. It would still be fun to check it out just a little while.

I'm standing there enjoying the atmosphere when Troy Nixon comes out onto the rear deck, looks around, and turns away to go back inside.

"Sorry to bother you," he tells me. "I was just looking for someone."

"No problem," I tell him. "I hope you find them."

He hesitates, arches his eyebrow, and gives me a look on the side. "Are you okay?"

"I'm fine. Donovan and I broke up. He got too jealous over the whole you incident."

Troy snorts. "It wouldn't be the first time someone got the wrong idea about me."

I have to smile at him. "I'm sure you get a lot of attention from the ladies."

"It isn't like I got a lot of attention from you. You only asked about your cousin. He had no reason to go off the deep end like that."

"It's for the best that I found out what he's like. I'm actually happy that we broke up."

He makes a face. "Are you really? Tell the truth."

"Well….no, but I'll be okay. It really is for the best. I know that now. I'm glad I found out about him before it got any more serious."

"Let me know if you need anything—or if he bothers you or anything. That's what I'm here for."

I start to say, "Thanks," when I spot Donovan passing through the piazza. Troy doesn't see him. Donovan is on his way from the elevators to the concourse.

He doesn't see me or Troy. Donovan can't see anything because he has his arm around another woman. He's just in the act of turning his head to smile at her inches away from her face.

That didn't take long. He's hitting on someone else less than twenty-four hours after breaking up with me.

Did he drum up this whole jealousy thing so he could run around with other people? I never thought he could be that belligerent, but maybe he had other reasons to make me think he was.

I shake that out of my head. Troy says he'll see me later and walks off down the breezeway toward the pools. He doesn't see Donovan before Donovan and his lady friend head into the concourse and disappear.

I turn my back on them and look out over the ocean. All this doubt and concern about Donovan—it's just a byproduct of the breakup being so fresh. It will all pass.

This is all confirmation that the breakup was the right thing to do. I didn't do it, but I would have if he didn't do it first.

I let myself relax in the rightness of this. I feel good. My life is good. My life will keep being good after I go back home.

This is just another breakup. It doesn't mean anything. He's the one with a problem. All I did was find out that Troy Nixon isn't my cousin. I never did anything wrong and neither did Troy.

I'm standing there with my head in the clouds when another person steps out onto the rear deck behind me. I don't even have the energy to pay attention when the curly-haired guy from the casino stops next to me.

"Hi," he greets me. "I'm Marco de Rossi. We met the other night in the casino."

I don't even look at him. "I remember who you are and I'm just as not interested now as I was then. You can keep moving."

"I'm not trying to hit on you. I told you that. I'm here with my girlfriend and planning to propose to her. I want to talk to you because I was wondering if you might be my sister."

My head snaps around and I find myself staring at him extra hard. "Your sister! How on Earth could I be your sister?!"

"My sister Becca fell off a fishing boat when she was six years old. They never found her body or any other evidence of her death. She just disappeared. My family has spent the last twenty-five years looking for her. We have computer-generated renderings of what she would look like now—and she looks like you. None of us have ever met anyone who looks as much like her as you do. I was wondering....if you might be her. I don't mean to intrude and I really don't mean to hit on you. Like I said, I'm here with someone else and she's already furious with me that I'm even talking to you."

My shoulders slump. "She has no reason to be. You have every right to find out if I'm your sister."

"So...you'll help me?"

"Sure. What do you want to know? Where are you from?"

"My family lives in Wichita Falls...."

"Really? Me, too! Small world, huh?"

He smiles. He has a nice smile, now that I understand he doesn't want to start something. "My sister disappeared in Florida. Have you ever been there?"

"Oh, sorry, no. I've never been to Florida, not even on vacation. I've spent my whole life in the Midwest."

"And....your family.....you never went boating.....or anything like that?"

I shake my head. "Sorry. I wish I could help you."

He turns away, but not before I see him wince. Ouch. This must hurt.

"I'm really sorry," I tell him. "I wish I could help."

"You did," he mumbles out the side of his mouth. "I should have known better than to get my hopes up. She's probably dead for all I know."

"Hey! Don't give up." I take a chance and lay my hand on his arm. "There's always hope until you hear that she really is dead. Stranger things have happened."

"You would think we would have found something after searching for so long." He grimaces again. "At least I didn't tell my parents about you. They would be destroyed if I told them and then they found out that you weren't Becca."

"Is your family okay?"

"They're fine. They're all trying to move on with their lives. We don't even talk about Becca anymore even though I know my parents are still looking. We all try to put it behind us, but it's always there, you know?"

I don't, but I can see how much it means to him. He keeps his head down and mumbles at the deck. He won't look up at me or anything else.

He speaks in such a defeated undertone that it breaks my heart. "I guess that's why this stings so much, you know? I was putting it behind me, too. I didn't even tell Angeline about it even though I'm planning to propose to her. The whole Becca thing just seemed so far in the past that there was no point in even bringing it up. I got it in my head that she was gone and never coming back, so I might as well just try to have a normal life without her. Then this happened and it all came back. I don't know....Maybe it will just take a while to get over the disappointment."

"And your fiancé doesn't understand? She doesn't support you?"

He shrugs at nothing. "She saw me staring at you at the safety briefing. She got jealous.....and then she doubted the whole story because I never mentioned Becca before. She'll be livid when she finds out I actually talked to you."

"That's terrible. You had every reason to talk to me. I'm glad you did. It would have eaten you up inside if you didn't find out one way or the other."

His head jerks up and his eyes lock on me with unbelievable power. He definitely sees me now. "That's what I said! I had to find out even if it cost the relationship. I mean....I couldn't face my family if I just let you walk away. You really might have been Becca—and then where would we be?"

"Exactly. Would it help if I talked to your fiancé?"

"No!" he blurts out and then fights himself under control. "No, I'll handle it. She won't have any reason to be jealous anymore once she finds out you aren't Becca. Please don't be offended if I have to pretend for the rest of the cruise like you don't exist. I'm sure she'll insist on that."

I have to laugh. "Okay. I won't be offended. I'll understand. I hope things quiet down for you."

His features soften and he smiles at me again. He looks much more relaxed now, too. "Thank you. You have no idea what this means."

"I do because you told me. I'm glad you asked. I really hope you find what you're looking for."

He stares at me for a minute and then turns away shaking his head. "The resemblance is uncanny. I'll see you around. Oh, wait." He turns back and holds out his hand. "I didn't catch your name."

"It's Jenn." I shake hands with him. "Jenn Hayworth."

"It's a pleasure to meet you. Thank you again. I'm really grateful—and thank you for listening. I guess...I won't see you around sometime."

I laugh again. "But I'll see you. Don't worry about it. I hope you have a good rest of the cruise."

"You, too. Tell your fella he's a lucky guy."

He walks off and leaves me with a million thoughts running through my head. I don't have a fella anymore, but Marco's words ring in my ears.

I'll find someone else to go out with. He'll be the lucky guy since Donovan obviously doesn't know what's good for him.

Chapter 7: Jenn

I wander back to my cabin—the cabin that's all mine now. I sit down on the couch and pick up the room service menu.

I don't feel like going down to the concourse to eat at a real restaurant. I might see Donovan and his new fling down there together. I definitely don't want that.

I'll have to leave this cabin and go socialize with real human beings at some point, but I won't do it now.

A woman showing up single at one of those places is bound to draw the sharks like blood in the water. I need to be ready for that.

The menu doesn't appeal to me, so I toss it back on the table. I'm going to have to get a whole lot hungrier before I go that far.

I pick up the TV streaming guide, but someone knocks on the door just then. It might be Troy asking about the jewel thieves again.

I go answer it and my shoulders stiffen when I find Donovan standing there. "Can I help you?" I ask in my frostiest tone.

"I left some stuff in the room," he replies in the same icy tone. "I need to get it out."

I step aside and wave into the cabin. He goes into the other bedroom, rummages around, and comes out putting something into the pocket of his jacket. I don't see what it is and I frankly do not care.

He clips, "Thanks," and breezes out as easily as he breezed in. He's probably on his way to a date with whatever-her-name-is.

I shut the door that he so rudely left open. Then I sink onto the couch again. It isn't like he brought so much excitement to my life, but I feel deflated after seeing him again. Life would be so much easier if I never saw him again.

I will see him again. We have to separate our stuff and move out of our apartment as soon as we get back home. That should be a laugh a minute.

I should rent another apartment while I'm still on the cruise. Then I won't have to live in the same apartment with him or even an apartment I once lived in with him. I can just go straight home to my new place.

I go into my room. It's all mine and always has been. I never shared it with him, so he never contaminated it with the need for me to remember our relationship.

I open my laptop to search for apartments when I get a notification that my mom is calling me. I click open my video chat app.

"Hi, Mom," I tell her. "How's everyone back home?"

"We're fine, darling," she replies and my dad comes over to sit in the camera frame with her.

"How are you and Donovan doing?" my dad asks.

I groan. "We broke up last night if you want to know the real truth."

My mom gasps and her hand flies to her mouth. "Oh, no! That's terrible! What happened?"

"I spotted a guy who looked like Flynn. I thought it was him and I wanted to talk to him to find out. Donovan just completely wigged out on me and stormed off. I just saw him with another girl a few hours ago—so I guess there's no moss gathering on that rolling stone."

"I can't believe it!" my dad exclaims. "You two were so happy to-gether."

"Maybe it's for the best."

He frowns. "What do you mean?"

"Never mind. I don't want to talk about it. Hey, you want to hear a strange story? Some guy came up to me on the boat today and said he thought I was his sister. He says his sister fell off a boat in Florida when she was six and this guy's family has been looking for her for twenty-five years. He says they have computer renderings of what she would look like and I look like her. Isn't that weird—me seeing someone who looks like Flynn and this guy seeing someone who looks like his missing sister? It's like some kind of cosmic convergence or something."

They both stare at me in stark horror and then my mom squirms. They both glance at each other.

"What's wrong?" I ask. "Don't worry about Donovan. He'll be fine and I'll be fine. This really was for the best. Trust me."

"It isn't that, darling." My mom's voice quavers. "It's just...."

I start to get a really bad feeling about this. "Something's wrong, isn't it? Did something happen after I left town?"

"No, nothing like that," my mom replies. "It's just....." She breaks off again.

"It's like this, sweetheart," my dad cuts in. "We....it's just...you're adopted, sweetheart. It's a long story, but the truth is that you suffered an accident when you were little. The Police found you with a head injury. It affected your memory. You had no idea who you were, where you were, or how you got there. No one even knew how old you were....so you see, sweetie.....it is conceivably possible that you are this man's sister."

I gape at him with my jaw on the floor. "I'm....I'm adopted?! Why didn't you tell me?"

"You were so messed up when you were little. It took you years to get your cognitive functions back. The doctors weren't even sure if you *would* get them back, but you did. It just took years. We all just tried to give you a normal life—as normal as possible. We just hoped you would come out of it and be able to think straight—because you couldn't before, you see—and you did in the end—and we're so proud of you. It just...it never came up, see? We never thought it would be an issue. The Police tried everything to find your family. They plastered your picture all over the country, but no one ever came forward to say they knew who you were. We figured.....if they couldn't find out who you were or where you came from, then there was no chance we could find out. We just let it go. I'm sorry, sweetie. We just tried to do the best thing for you—and it just seemed better to let you go along the way you were. Things were hard enough for you back then. We didn't want to make it harder than it already was."

He trails off. My mom's lips quiver as she holds back tears.

My mind starts whirling in a million directions. I could be Marco's sister after all.

I don't blame my parents for keeping this from me. It explains so many things.

I never could remember much from before I was about seven. My memory was notoriously terrible even after that.

I remember those years. It seemed so hard just to think straight like my dad says. Everyone else I knew—everyone at school—they all seemed to be able to think so much better than I could.

My teachers were always really nice about it and patient with my forgetfulness. My parents must have told them that I was recovering from a head injury.

I have to tell Marco about this. I can't leave him and his family in any doubt about where we stand. They have a right to know about me even if I don't turn out to be Becca.

"Please don't hold this against us, sweetheart." Now my dad's voice starts to shake.

My mom bursts into tears and my dad winds up holding her. Even my dad has tears in his eyes when he turns back to the screen.

"We'll send you the adoption paperwork," he chokes. "You can go over it with this guy and figure out what's what."

"Okay, Dad. I love you. I don't hold it against either of you. I'm grateful for the life you gave me. You're the only parents I'll ever have—and the only family I'll ever have. I don't hold anything against you."

That makes my mom cry even harder. Tears streak down my dad's cheeks. Did they really think I would turn against them because of this? Why on Earth would I do that?

"I better go, Dad. I love you. I gotta go talk to Marco about this. You and Mom take care of yourselves."

"Okay, sweetheart," my dad husks. "We love you. I'll send the paperwork to you as soon as possible."

"Thank you," I tell him. "I'm sure Marco's family will be grateful, too."

He's too emotional to answer with anything other than a nod. He hangs up without saying goodbye.

I slam my laptop shut, toss the computer on the bed, and leap to my feet. I have to talk to Marco right now. I rush out of the room and head for the elevator.

Chapter 8: Marco

I walk around the ship for a long time, lean over isolated parts of the railing, and stare off at the horizon for a long time.

Jenn. Jenn Hayworth.

She isn't my sister Becca after all. Finding that out is almost worse than losing Becca the first time. It's going to take me a while to get over this.

I dread going back to the cabin and seeing Angeline again. She won't act all understanding and sympathetic. She has no clue that I'm grieving over this as much as I'm grieving over my sister's loss.

How did I get myself saddled with such an unfeeling, uncaring, hostile woman? What was I ever thinking when I planned to marry her?

Jenn was a lot more understanding. She was so kind.

That's the real kicker in this. A total stranger was kinder to me than the woman I was planning to make my fiancé.

I should go break up with her right this minute, but I'm too bruised about losing.....Jenn. She isn't Becca.

The worst thing is that I'll never be able to talk to Jenn again as long as Angeline is around. I'll have to avoid Jenn—the one person in all of this who actually cares and understands.

What I wouldn't give to talk to her. I wish I could pour out my soul to her. I already did and she understands. She knows this hurts.

Angeline just doesn't care. She only cares about how I hurt her with this whole thing when I didn't.

She's totally self-centered. That's what this means. She's incapable of seeing this from my point of view. She only cares about herself.

I won't break up with her now. I'll wait until my mind clears and I'm not so wrapped up in this.

I stay out a lot longer than I planned. I need to think by myself.

The ocean gives me a perfect place to do that. I can pretend I'm alone out here instead of trapped on a boat with thousands of other people.

The sun rises higher getting closer to the zenith before I'm ready to interact with anyone. I guess I better go deal with her.

I savor the last minutes of quiet while I ride up the elevator. None of these people know what I'm going through. None of these people know the universe just delivered a brutal smackdown on my life.

They all see me walking around. They all see me acting normally. They think I am normal when I'm really bleeding from an amputated limb.

Losing Becca felt like this. It didn't stop bleeding for years. Christ, I hope I don't go through that again.

I just have to keep going no matter what else happens. I have nothing else to do with this wreck of a life.

I slow down when I approach the suite I share with Angeline. I really don't want to go in there, but I have to face the music.

I walk inside and see her standing on the balcony. She gazes off toward the sun. It shines on her face, her long flowing blonde hair, and reflects off her round, flushed cheeks.

I go out there and slip my arm around her waist when I ease up to her and lean on the railing. "How was your day?"

"It was great. This ship has everything."

"Yeah, it does," I murmur. I can't even talk to her.

"I really like this balcony," she goes on. "You can see almost the entire ship from up here."

I look around. She's right. We can see almost the entire ship—on this side anyway.

"And look right down there." She points below us. "You can see everything happening on the rear deck right there. Isn't that interesting?"

I look down at the rear deck directly below us. The whole truth comes into my mind with crystal clarity. She saw us. Angeline must have been standing here watching me talking to Jenn.

I turn away and walk back into the cabin. I don't have to deal with this.

"I told you not to mess around with her," she calls after me. "You just don't listen."

"I wasn't messing around with her," I reply over my shoulder. "I was asking her about Becca."

"And? Is she your long-lost make-believe sister?"

I don't take the bait. "No, she isn't. Becca disappeared in Florida and Jenn is from Wichita Falls just like we are. She's spent her whole life in the Midwest. She's never been to Florida and neither has her family."

"There you go," she snaps. "Now you have no reason to ever talk to her again."

"I wasn't planning to."

Silence falls over the room. She doesn't chime in with any more biting comments about Becca being make-believe. How could anyone be so callous?

I could never let this woman around my family. That was a giant mistake I can never repeat. I can't risk her saying something like that around my parents—or anyone else in my family.

It's bad enough she's saying them to me, but it doesn't matter. Every word out of her mouth just seals the end of our relationship.

I go into my room and take off my shirt to change for dinner. I don't really care where we go or what we do. I feel numb to everything.

She finally comes inside, enters my room, and comes up behind me. She slips her arms around my waist, kisses me on the back of the shoulder, and sits down on my bed.

"What do you want to do today?" she asks.

"You pick," I tell her.

She smirks at me. "I asked you first."

I shrug at nothing. She's too into herself to notice how flat I'm acting.

She doesn't think she's going to waltz back into my life and pretend none of this ever happened. I think not.

I'm staying in this room apart from her because she couldn't accept the story about Becca. She tried to punish me for wanting answers about my missing sister. That's why we're staying in separate rooms.

She pushed me away and sent me over to this room like a badly behaved dog. She doesn't seriously think I would forget about that, does she?

"We could go down to the concourse, get some lunch, and see what we feel like doing after that," I tell her.

She bounces off the bed and flounces to the door. "I'm going to get ready."

"I'm gonna go down to the store and get another tube of tooth-paste," I tell her. "I'll be back in a few minutes."

She spins around and stares at me. She has the tube of toothpaste in her room—the tube of toothpaste we share as a couple. She kept it when she threw me out.

Now maybe she'll understand that I don't plan to just take her back without a squeak of protest. I can go get a new tube of toothpaste. I don't need her for that.

I definitely don't need the aggravation of dealing with someone who's gonna play these stupid games with me. I put on a clean shirt and go down to the concourse.

I buy my toothpaste and put it in my pocket, but I don't want to go back upstairs and deal with her again. She can sit there and think about it for a while. I don't need to be the one to make up with her—not after she was the one who fouled the nest.

I go into one of the nearby restaurants, sit down at the bar, and order a sandwich. I don't feel like eating lunch with Angeline—not today. I want to drown my sorrows in food.

The bartender puts a set of silverware wrapped in a napkin in front of me so I'm ready when my order comes out.

I'm just considering ordering something to drink—something non-alcoholic. I don't want to start drowning my sorrows for real when it's still only lunchtime.

Loud voices interrupt my thoughts just then. I turn around to see Jenn's boyfriend or fiancé or husband or whatever he is getting in Troy Nixon's face.

A guy would have to have a death wish to get in that guy's face. Troy always acts so calm, but anyone can feel the danger simmering just below the surface.

I don't know the guy's background. I don't want to know, but it must be something pretty serious. I would bet cold hard cash he can get dangerous when he wants to be—or needs to be—like now.

"I hope you're happy, asshole," the guy fumes. I don't even know his name. "You just had to go and mess everything up, but that's okay. I'm going to file a complaint with the cruise line and get you thrown out on your ass where you belong."

Troy answers in his usual calm, unruffled voice. "You can call me all the names you want, Mr. McNulty. I didn't do anything to you or Jenn. I never did anything other than my job—but you already knew that. Now take a step back and lower your voice or we're going to start having a problem here."

The guy doesn't back off. He's too stupid to see Troy bracing himself for the worst.

The guy chest bumps Troy again. "I'm talking to you, asshole! How many other passengers and the passengers' wives have you been banging on the side? Huh? I really want to know!"

Troy drops his voice into the danger zone. "None, Mr. McNulty. I have never done it with any passenger and I never looked sideways at Jenn. I have no interest in her or any other passenger."

"You're a lying sack of shit! You would lie about anything to cover up what a player you are!"

Troy doesn't have to lift a finger. A dozen security guards swoop out of nowhere, grab the dude, and haul him out of the restaurant.

He struggles and yells curses, insults, and threats over his shoulder as they drag him away. Don't even ask me what they plan to do with him.

Chapter 9: Marco

I head back upstairs with my stomach full. I plan to tell Angeline that I'm not hungry and just want to hang out in the suite. She can go down to the concourse and get lunch by herself. I hope she enjoys herself.

I don't know what I'll do instead. Maybe I'll watch a movie or something to take my mind off of all of this.

I find the suite empty. She's already gone. Hopefully she's out getting lunch with someone else—someone whose company she enjoys more than mine.

I plunk down on the couch and pick up the streaming guide, but a knock on the door interrupts me. It can't be Angeline coming back. She has a key. She wouldn't knock.

My stomach drops when I see Jenn standing outside. "Uh....what's up?" I ask.

She shuffles her feet and looks all around her in squirming agitation. "I'm really sorry!" she blurts out. "I need to talk to you! I know I said I would understand if you had to avoid me—but it's important—like really important! I wouldn't be here if it wasn't."

"Okay." I wave behind me. "Come on in."

She storms into the cabin and starts pacing around extra fast. I don't know what to do or say. "Um....do you want to sit down....or do you want something to drink....?"

"I'm adopted!" she blurts out. "My parents never told me! They don't know where I came from! I had a head injury when I was young—and they don't even know how old I was when the Police found me! I had no memory of anything that happened or where I came from or even what my name was! They searched the whole country and never found my family! My parents say the injury affected my memory for years—so I could be Becca! Don't you see, Marco?! I could be Becca after all!"

I freeze as those words stab me in the guts. I don't want to believe it. "What if.....?" I stammer.

"My parents are sending me all the adoption paperwork! I don't know what to do!" She waves her arms around her head. She won't stop pacing even for an instant. "This could be...I mean.....you could be my brother.....and I could have a whole family I don't know about.....my parents.....they both broke down in tears when they told me.....they think I'm going to turn against them because of this! Can you believe that? I don't know what to do about all this.....!"

Seeing her so agitated finally brings me back to Earth. Someone is more distressed about this than I am.

I take a step forward and grab her hand. "Hey!" I murmur. "It's okay. Come here. Sit down. You don't need to figure it all out. Everything's gonna work out. We'll figure it out, okay?"

She has a hard time listening to me and an even harder time sitting down. I have to pull her down in front of me.

"Listen to me," I murmur. "You're gonna get your adoption paperwork and then we'll see if you're Becca or not. If you aren't, then it's no big deal. You'll keep going on the way you have been and so will we.

Nothing will change. If you are, then my family will be over the moon and we'll all be thrilled to meet you and get to know you. You live in Wichita Falls and we live in Wichita Falls, so it will be easy for us to see each other whenever we feel like it and for us to arrange times that both of us feel comfortable with. None of us will try to stop you from being a part of your adoptive family. None of us wants to intrude on your life. None of us wants to make you uncomfortable at all. That isn't what this is about."

She looks up at me and immediately looks away. I see in that split-second glance how much this upsets her—not the part about finding out she's adopted.

She's upset because of what this might do to her family. She's upset that finding this out hurt her parents.

They must have taken really good care of her. It must have taken a truly special couple to adopt a child with that kind of injury. They loved her and helped her grow into this beautiful woman sitting in front of me.

I can't help but squeeze her hands. My sister. I love her already. I feel such a connection with her. I want to put my arms around her and welcome her back into my family after so many years gone.

Just sitting here across from her heals something that was broken in me. She's the missing piece of me—of all of us.

She pulls her hand out of mine so she can pass it upward across her forehead. She's so nervous and upset and confused about all of this. I love her for that.

"I'm really sorry—about earlier!" Her voice breaks with painful emotion.

"Why are you sorry? You were so kind to me."

"I mean....I'm sorry I told you the wrong thing! I know it hurt you when I said I never went to Florida—and now this......I just don't want you to go through that again—but I had to tell you! I couldn't let you not find out! I hope you understand....."

"Of course I understand. You're such a good person for talking to me earlier and now telling me about this. I'm so grateful for your help even though it's hard for you."

I barely get the words out before the door swings open and Angeline waltzes in. She takes one look at me sitting in front of Jenn holding her hand. Anyone can see Angeline's expression change in an instant.

"I knew it!" she rages. "I knew it—and you had to bring it here, didn't you? You couldn't keep it in your pants even for a few seconds! Get the hell out of here, you skank-ass tramp!"

I shoot off the couch in a flash. "Don't you dare talk to her like that! She came here to help me—which is a hell of a lot more than you've ever done!"

Jenn gets to her feet. "I'm really sorry! I just had to tell him....."

"You had to go behind my back and steal my man 'cuz you're such a gutter whore that you couldn't get one of your own!" Angeline storms. "You could have fucked him in a public bathroom and sent him on his way—but no! You had to come right on into my house and do it right here in front of my face!"

"I swear to God, Angeline, if you don't shut the hell up, I don't know what I'll do!" I interrupt. "She came up here to tell me that she might be my sister after all!"

"Do you think I give a shit why she's here—after all the shit you pulled on me?!" Angeline waves her index finger in my face and weaves her head back and forth. When did she turn into such a harpy?

Jenn whimpers one more time, "I'm really sorry!" and runs out of the room. I've heard enough.

"How dare you?!" I yell back at Angeline. "How dare you talk to her like that?! She could be my sister! Is that the way you talk to my family?"

"I talk to that bitch any way I want to! You said you wouldn't have anything else to do with her...."

"I said that because we thought she wasn't my sister—and you didn't even have the decency to understand why I had to find out! What is the matter with you?! You said you would be there for me—and you turned against me the minute I needed you. Is this the relationship we've been in all this time? Are you so pig-headed that you would talk to someone in my family like that—and you had the nerve to call Becca make-believe?! Do you honestly think I would waste my time with someone who would treat me with such colossal disrespect!"

"We aren't in a relationship! Do you got that!" She barges over to her bedroom. "We're done!"

"Good!" I yell after her. "I'm done with you, too! I have no use for someone who could treat me the way you have these last few days!"

"You deserve it!" Her voice comes from inside the room. I hear her banging around in there. "You were gawking at her right in front of me—and I saw you practically making out with her on the rear deck!"

"I was not making out with her! I was talking to her! Now you're making up lies to defend yourself! I never flirted with her—and now I find out she could be my sister! Why can't you pull your head out of your ass long enough to see that?"

"I don't have to listen to this!" she bellows. "I'm leaving!"

"Good!" I snap. "Don't let the doorknob hit you in the ass on the way out."

I don't want to say anything else and I don't want to let her get the last word. I go into my room, shut, and lock the door until I hear her leave.

Then I go down to the purser's office and ask for a new key to that suite. I tell them Angeline moved out, take her name off the booking agreement, and turn in my old key. She won't be able to get back in.

Chapter 10: Jenn

I stand at the entrance to the concourse and stare at all the people walking around. They drink in the bars, eat in the restaurants, gamble in the casinos, watch shows, listen to bands, attend plays and musicals, laugh at comedians, and shop in all the stores.

I don't know what to do first, but I guess I have to do something. I wander down the concourse and finally decide to bite the bullet and go into a bar.

I'm all dressed up to go out. I look like I'm about to go on a date except that I don't have one.

I sit down at the bar and order a drink. Then I decide to order dinner because why not? I'm on a date with myself.

Troy comes in and stands at the bar to check in with the bartenders. He makes a regular circuit of all the establishments on the ship. All the security guys do, but he has to talk to all the staff and crew to make sure everything is under control.

The guy must have an insane job, but he's so good at it. He spots me sitting there alone. "You okay?" he asks.

"I'm fine. I'm newly single, so this is me dipping my toe into the shallow end of the pool."

"Good idea. You know where my office is if you need anything."

"Thanks. Let's hope I never see you there."

He laughs. "Yeah. I wouldn't want that."

I smile at him before he leaves. What a great guy. Of course he's married. He's too good to be single.

I turn back to my meal when a guy comes up to the bar. He's here to order a drink. He gets interested when he sees me alone. "Hello," he greets me. "Are you here by yourself?"

"Yes, I'm on a date with myself."

He laughs and takes a step closer. "I wouldn't want to interrupt that."

I smile at him. "I'm very good company for myself."

"Is there room for a third on this date?"

"There might be, but only if the person is as good company as I am."

He sits down on the stool next to me. "What is your date drinking?"

"My date doesn't drink. My date is a lightweight, so I'm doing the drinking for both of us."

He laughs again. "Are you on the cruise by yourself, too?"

"No, I came with my boyfriend, but we broke up the very first night—so now I'm on the cruise by myself. So I guess the answer to your question is yes."

"Ouch," he exclaims. "That's pretty rough—breaking up the very first night."

"Actually it worked out for the best. I'm a much better date than he is anyway."

He sticks out his hand. "I'm Steve—Steve Bartlett."

I shake his hand. "Jenn Hayworth. Nice to meet you."

He leans a little closer. "Do you and your date have plans for after dinner?"

I open my mouth, but right at that minute, a woman in a tight red dress barges up to the bar, grabs Steve by his jacket collar, and drags him off his stool.

"How many times do I have to tell you?!" the woman thunders. "I am so gonna kick your ass when we get back to the room!"

I watch them out of sight and turn back to the bar just as the bartender puts my food in front of me. So much for that.

I'm going to have to watch out for people like that, now that I'm single.

I finish my meal without further incident. Most of the people on the cruise are part of a couple and much better behaved than our good friend Steve. No one else hits on me all evening—so I'm winning.

I decide to quit while I'm ahead. I dipped my toe into the shallow end of the pool. I call it an early night and head back toward the elevator.

Everyone is on the concourse or out on the deck at this time of night. I have the elevator to myself.

I ride up to my deck planning to crawl into bed and maybe veg out with a movie or something. I can't handle anything more complicated than that.

The elevator dings and I rummage in my purse for my room key. I'm just turning the corner when I hear banging ahead.

I don't think anything of it and continue toward my room when I happen to pass a broom and mop closet on this deck. The door stands open and I look straight in at a man and a woman doing it against the wall.

The woman has her skirt hitched up to her waist, her bare thighs strapped around the guy's hips, and the guy has his pants around his knees while he pounds her against the wall.

The woman keeps her arms hugged tightly around his neck and he gasps and pants, "Oh, baby! Oh, baby!" into her ear again and again.

I can't see her face behind his head and I don't want to. I'm just about to walk away when she loosens her grip, pulls back enough to face him, and they kiss once before they go back to panting in each other's mouths.

I get a clear look at the woman's face. It's Angeline, Marco's girlfriend.

I hustle away before they see me, but the sight triggers another hurricane of anxiety in me. How am I ever supposed to face Marco with this hanging over my head?

He could be my brother. I could be intimately involved with his whole family from now on.

I would never be able to look him in the eye knowing his girlfriend was cheating on him. He even said he was planning to propose to her.

I would be intimately involved with Angeline, too. I would have to see her at family get-togethers—the woman that called me a skank and a whore.

I can't stand still, but I don't dare to go back the way I came. I take the stairs down to the rear deck and stand there with my face turned into the salt spray so I can clear my head.

I have to decide what to do about this. I have to decide before I see Marco again. I can't even look at my email before I decide if I'm going to tell him or not.

Of course I'm going to tell him. I have to tell him. That isn't a question. We're family—or we might be.

I owe him that much. I've already confided my most dangerous secret to him. I couldn't keep this from him.

This affects him a hell of a lot more than it affects me. He's been living with the unknown about Becca's fate all these years.

This is the woman in his life. He has to know, especially if he plans to marry her.

Just don't ask me how I'm going to tell him, especially after all those terrible names she called me. She already hates me. What if she denies it and calls me a liar?

The sea spray makes me cold. I won't do anything tonight. I might as well go to my room after all.

I decide to take the stairs again. I don't want to see anyone I know. I won't see anyone I know once I get to my suite. I can lock the door and refuse to see anyone ever again. Maybe that's for the best.

I turn around to walk back inside. The shadows trick my eyes and I wind up colliding with another person coming out onto the rear deck from inside.

I scream out loud when I see that the person is Marco. He grabs my arms to steady me. "Easy!" he tells me. "It's just me."

I struggle against his grip and he lets go and raises his hands. "Take it easy," he tells me. "I wasn't going to hurt you."

"Marco!" I practically shriek.

"Yeah," he breathes. "It's just me."

"Angeline....."

His face turns black and his voice drops to a snarl. Does he already know? "What about her? She won't ever call you those names again. I promise."

"She....." I have to tell him.

"She what?" he snaps. "She better not have come after you."

"No....she.....she was in the broom closet....with another guy.....just now....."

He stares at me with the same fierce glare and then his whole expression melts. He relaxes and his face clears. "Oh. Okay."

"You...you knew?!"

"No, no. I didn't know, but I'm not surprised."

"You aren't?!" I practically bellow. "How can you not be surprised?! You said you were going to propose to her!"

"We just broke up—right after you left. We split up because she got so over-the-top out of her mind about this whole Becca thing. She called Becca make-believe—and then after she blew up at you....well, it just had to end. It's for the best."

Those words snap me out of my hysteria. "You...you think so?"

He nods. "I know so. It's better that I found out about her now before I actually married her. That's okay. She can go out there and sleep with anyone she wants now. I don't care. They can have her."

I blink up at him. I really feel like he could be my brother.

He notices and smiles at me. "Are you okay?"

"I....I guess......I thought....I wasn't sure....what to do....I knew I had to tell you....I just didn't know how. I thought.....I didn't want to make it harder for you."

He takes my hand and leads me to one of the benches on the rear deck. "Sit down. We didn't get to finish talking before."

I sink onto the bench next to him. His hands feel warm. They help calm me down.

He really is like my brother. He always checks to make sure I'm okay. I feel relaxed and comfortable around him. I feel like I've known him all my life even though we just met.

"Are you okay—really—with this whole Becca thing?" he asks. "We can drop it if it's causing you so much distress."

"No! I want to! I wouldn't do that to your family." I look up at him. "I'm okay with it. I feel like....I don't know....It's crazy...but it's almost like I already feel like you're my brother. I feel like....like we're family."

He bursts into a huge grin. "I feel the same way. I feel like I love you—as a sister, I mean."

I find myself smiling back at him. "Yeah. Me, too."

"Maybe that's what Angeline saw when I was looking at you and talking to you. Maybe she saw that.....I love you....you know? Maybe she mistook it for something it wasn't—but it was still love."

I blush and try to look away, but my eyes always migrate back to him. "Yeah." I squeeze his hands. "I feel the same way."

He won't stop beaming at me. "I can't wait for you to meet my family. They are gonna be so proud of you—just like I am. It's amazing that you grew up the way you did after everything you went through when you were little."

Those words make me frown. "Your family....they won't resent me for sticking with my own family, will they? I mean....I don't want anyone else to be my mom and dad. I couldn't do that to them."

"No way!" he exclaims. "They're the ones who were there for you. You should stick with them. We all understand that. We just want to know what happened to you....I mean, if you are Becca."

"Of course. We shouldn't get ahead of ourselves until we know for sure."

He gazes deep into my eyes. "Would it be all right if I gave you a hug?"

"Sure!" I tell him. "Come here, big brother."

We hug each other and he breaks into happy laughter. He pushes me back and I see tears glistening in his eyes. I barely know the guy, but he looks so unbelievably happy.

He runs his hand across his nose. "I better get out of here before I make a fool of myself."

"Never," I tell him. "I'll come see you as soon as I get the adoption paperwork from my parents."

"Thanks." He smirks at me. "I can't wait."

I have to smile and he hurries away. Wow. That was like no interaction I've ever had in my life. I'm really starting to hope I am Becca.

I can't wait to meet his family. They must all be nice people if he turned out like this.

Chapter 11: Marco

I go back upstairs walking on a cloud. I love Jenn so much! She's so beautiful and pure, both inside and out.

Of course she told me about Angeline—and of course Angeline called Jenn a skank. Angeline said the word she knows she is.

We barely broke up a few hours ago and she's already nailing some dude in a broom closet. That is the skankiest thing I have ever heard of.

I get to my cabin and find her leaning her shoulder against the door. She's inspecting her fingernails while she waits for me.

"My key doesn't work," she tells me. "Something is wrong with it."

"Nothing is wrong with it. I changed the code so you can't get in. We broke up, remember?"

"I'm still booked in this room. I'm staying here for the rest of the cruise."

"No, you aren't," I counter. "You said you were leaving and you left. What's the matter? Is that the stain of some other guy's jiz in your panties right now?"

Her face drains of all color. "What did you say?" she husks.

"You just smashed some dude in the broom closet down the hall, didn't you? I hope he was good. Now I know what you're really made of."

"I did not!" she fires back. "That's a bald-faced lie."

I snort at her. "Please. Jenn saw you and told me. Just admit it. It's okay. I don't care. You can go bend over for any guy you want. You're as free as a bird."

Her expression hardens in front of my eyes. "So Jenn told you!" she sneers. "She's a lying cunt. She would make up any lie to steal you from me."

My blood starts to boil, but I fight my temper under control with a heroic effort. "I told you not to call her that. She's a hell of a lot nicer than you are."

"She lied about being your sister and she's lying about this."

I glare at her in pure hatred. I never thought I could hate someone this much. "She is my sister. Go on. Go sleep with half of Seattle for all I care. At least some guys will have a good time into the bargain."

She clamps her mouth shut and narrows her eyes at me. "You'll find out I'm right and then you'll see what a con artist she is. You're a chump if you believe her story."

She struts off down the hall. Her ass looks as great as ever in her tight skirt, but all I can think is that some other guy just had her.

I hope he liked it because I will never go near her again. Her sleeping around mere minutes after our breakup is nowhere near as bad as her bad-mouthing Jenn right to my face.

I go inside and go to bed. At least Angeline can't get back into the room.

I don't know where she'll spend the night tonight. I'm sure some lonely dishwasher down in the kitchens will let her share his bed tonight. She deserves it.

I wake up the next morning, go out onto the balcony, and immediately start to doubt everything I felt last night.

What if Angeline is right and Jenn is playing me? What if she made up that adoption story and the story about Angeline sleeping around?

Jenn didn't make up the part about Angeline turning hostile just because I wanted to find out who Jenn was. Jenn didn't make up the part about Angeline throwing me out of the bedroom.

I really need some answers. So where can I get them?

I wander around the ship at loose ends. I don't know whether I'm coming or going until I spot Troy Nixon.

He's up early wearing casual business attire, going from one establishment to another, and checking in with everyone. The grass doesn't grow long under that guy's feet.

His eyes go hard when he spots me watching him and he comes over to me. "Marco de Rossi, isn't it?" he asks.

"Yes, Sir," I tell him. "In the flesh."

"I'm Troy Nixon. I'm Chief of Security for the *Electric Emerald.*"

"Yes, Sir. I know who you are. Everyone knows who you are."

He gives me a hard look. "Are you ex-military or something?"

"No, Sir, but my dad is. I guess you could say I got into the habit of addressing everyone that way when they're in a position of authority."

He bursts out in a huge grin. "I'm not in a position of authority."

"Excuse me, Sir, but yes, you are. You're the ultimate authority on this ship."

He laughs. "In that case, maybe you wouldn't mind showing me your passport. I need to check that you have all the necessary visas for all your shore visits."

"Yes, Sir. No problem." I pull my passport out of my wallet and hand it over.

He checks it, takes a photo of the visas with his phone, and hands the passport back. "Thank you. It's really nice when the passengers cooperate."

"Yes, Sir. You won't have any trouble with me."

He smiles at me. "Feel free to let me know if you need help with anything of a security nature. That's what I'm here for."

I open my mouth and stop myself from asking. Maybe I shouldn't.

He's too smart not to notice my hesitation. "What?" he asks. "What is it?"

"I was just wondering.....It's just....someone accused my girlfriend of cheating on me. She denies it. I was wondering....if you could somehow help me find the proof.....like maybe you have security camera footage of the location and all that. Is that something you can do.....or is it confidential?"

"No, that is definitely something I can do. Follow me. I'm on my way back to the office now. We can do it there."

My heart leaps when I follow him back to the security office. It looks tiny from the outside, but it opens into multiple rooms and other offices in the back.

He goes into a large office in the very back, steps behind a desk, taps on the mouse for a minute, does something on his phone, and then leads the way to the security camera room.

Dozens of monitors cover one wall. Three different guards sit in there watching everything.

Troy exchanges a few words with the other guys, sits down, and starts working on a different station. "Where do they say she did it?"

"In a broom closet," I reply. "That's all I know."

He works on the computer for a few minutes and brings up the footage for a bunch of different broom closets. There must be dozens all over the ship.

"*When* do they say it happened?" he asks.

"Sometime last night—around nine o'clock, I'd say."

He works in silence for a little longer before he locates some footage of Jenn standing in the hall. I leap forward and point. "There! That's her! That's the person who saw them. The broom closet must be near there."

I can't breathe as he maneuvers the cameras in different directions. He finally angles them so he captures the footage inside the closet.

All my agitation dies in a blink when I see the guy standing with his pants down and his hips thrusting between Angeline's legs. It's all real. Of course Jenn wouldn't lie to me. She saw the whole thing.

I turn away feeling sick. Why on God's green Earth did I ever doubt Jenn's word? How did I let Angeline get into my head like this?

She betrayed me once. She betrayed me twice. She betrayed me more times than I can count.

Why would I think for two seconds that she wouldn't lie to me about this, too? What was I thinking that I believed in her again?

I wander out of the room, but I can't bring myself to leave this office. How can I keep taking these hits? Where's the limit where I just can't take anymore?

At least I know now. I know who and what she really is. I don't have to wonder anymore.

I stand at the window looking out at the ocean. I need to be out there at the ship's rail where I can think. These walls confine me. I can't clear my head as long as I'm in here, but this realization keeps me frozen. I can't move.

Troy comes up behind me and stands next to me. "You'll be okay," he tells me. "Just confront her with the truth, call it a day, and move on. She isn't worth any more of your time than that. Here. Take this." He hands me a memory stick. "The footage is on here. You can use this to prove she was lying. Then you can get her out of your life for good and never look back."

The memory stick feels real in my hand. I have something real to hold onto—something that proves I'm not making a big deal out of nothing.

I finally work up the mental power to leave the security office and go back up to my suite. I'm just walking in the door when Angeline shows up. She darts inside before the door closes.

She grins at me. "Well? What's the plan for today?"

"We're going to watch a movie together," I tell her.

She brightens up. "Cool! Which movie is it?"

"It's a surprise." I get my laptop out of my room, sit down on the couch, boot up the machine, and plug in the memory stick.

She sits down next to me, curls her legs under her, drapes her arm over my shoulder, and cuddles up to me like we're on a date or something.

The memory stick only has one file on it. I open the file and the footage starts playing. The footage even includes the image of Jenn watching from out in the hall.

The footage shows her coming out of the elevator and digging in her purse for her key. There's no way she knew Angeline was in there spreading her legs for another guy. Jenn just happened to be walking by.

Angeline stiffens on the couch next to me. Then, without warning, she leaps away. "You tricked me, Marco!"

"Actually, you were the one who lied to me. You said you didn't screw around with that guy and then you tried to spin me a story about Jenn conning me with this. What is wrong with you that you could mess with my head like that?"

She rushes back to the couch, sits down, and tries to snuggle up to me again. "I'm sorry!" she wheedles. "I was confused! I got emotional after we had a fight and I just needed to blow off steam...."

I push her away a lot harder than I should. I launch off the couch and take my laptop with me. "Don't you dare touch me! Keep away from me!"

"I'm sorry!!" she exclaims and stands up to follow me, but at least she doesn't come near me. "We can work this out. What we have is too good to let something like this ruin it."

I gape at her and blink in shock. "Too good! You call this too good?! You turned against me and threw me out of the bedroom for trying to find my sister. My sister, Angeline! The sister my whole family has been searching for for the last twenty-five years! You got nasty and threatened our relationship because you were too selfish to support me when I needed you. You said you would always back me up and be there for me—and then you turned on me the very first time something didn't revolve around you—and then you split up with me for the crime of even talking to Jenn—and then you went and banged some other guy—in a broom closet no less—and then you had the nerve to lie about it and blame Jenn—again! What the hell do you say is so good about this relationship?! There is no relationship! She's my sister! You destroyed our relationship for nothing! You don't care about me! You never cared about me! You only care about yourself! Now get the hell out of my cabin before I call security to remove you."

"No, Marco!" she chokes. "Don't do this! Give me another chance! I swear I'll make it up to you."

All my anger dies in that moment. I know exactly who and what I'm looking at right now.

"No," I tell her. "We're done. It's over—and you were the one who ended it. Just remember that when you're bending over for the next guy who wants a piece."

I put my laptop on the table, remove the memory stick, and walk out of the cabin. I don't need to deal with her now or ever again.

I go downstairs, check in with both the purser and Troy, and make absolutely certain Angeline is booked into another room.

I make it clear that we aren't staying in the same cabin anymore and Troy confirms that, if she comes back again, I can call security to have her removed.

He also tells me that he'll talk to her and warn her to stay away from me and Jenn. If Angeline violates that, she could get thrown off the ship.

Chapter 12: Jenn

I come downstairs clutching my laptop in shaking hands. I take it to a passenger observation lounge on the ship's topmost deck.

Marco is already there. He stands up from one of the couches when I walk in.

He gives me a hug and then peers deep into my eyes while he rubs the side of my arm. "Are you ready for this?"

"Not really, but we need to find out the truth. I'm ready whenever you are."

"I'm ready, too." He pulls me backward. "Come sit down."

We both sit down on the couch. I'm a nervous wreck.

He won't stop rubbing my back and stroking the hair out of my face. "Everything is gonna be fine no matter what the outcome is," he tells me. "You understand that, right?"

I nod and gulp. "Yeah. I'm just really nervous."

"Me, too—but whatever the outcome, it will be for the best. We both know that."

I nod. "Right. I know."

He glances down at the laptop. "Open it and let's find out. Let's get it over with."

I sit back, open my laptop, and open my email account. The email from my dad sits right there at the top. I haven't even had the nerve to open it yet.

I click on it and read my dad's message. "My dad says he hopes this answers my questions. He says he and my mom love me no matter what."

"There. You see?" Marco points out. "Nothing to worry about."

"I just hope everything is okay for your family, too."

"It will be. This can't tell us anything that can possibly make it worse. That's what you have to remember. This can only be good for us."

"Okay. Here we go." I click on the attachment to the email.

It opens a zipped folder of documents. The first is my adoption certificate.

Marco points to the date of birth. "That can't be your real birthdate if they didn't know how old you were."

"That's my birthday—or what I think is my birthday. The authorities must have just guessed at it so they could put something on the form. The birthplace says, 'unknown'—and the birth parents are listed as unknown."

"We already knew that. Open the next document. It's a Police report. That should tell us something."

I close the adoption certificate, open the Police report, and start reading.

"This lists the date as twenty-six years ago." I do some quick mental calculations. "I would have been about six and a half. 'Female child, dark brown hair, brown eyes, unknown age, found dazed, conscious, and unresponsive to verbal commands in Holliston Park, 4pm. The child was found with a gash and contusion to the upper right forehead. The gash extends into her scalp. She was unable to answer officers' questions about her name, origins, or the nature of her accident. The child was transported to the Emergency Department where she was admitted to the head injury clinic for treatment. The case was transferred to Missing Persons where the child's fingerprints and DNA were logged into the database, but no matches were found. The nationwide alert system was activated without results.'"

"Where's Holliston Park?" Marco asks.

"I'm not sure, but the report is from the Gary, Indiana, Police Department. Just give me a second."

I switch over to my internet browser and do a search for, *Holliston Park, Gary, Indiana.* The search brings up a Google map of the park. It's right there in the middle of Gary.

I turn to look up at Marco. "Gary, Indiana....I was found in Gary, Indiana."

His expression clears when he looks straight down into my eyes from inches away. "That's it, then. You can't be Becca. No way could she have gotten from Florida to Indiana in that time."

I don't look away and neither does he. I find myself staring all the way into his soul.

We both got so invested in this idea that I was his sister and he was my brother. He actually said he loved me as a sister—and I felt the same way.

It isn't true. I'm not Becca. I can't be.

Now I feel like I just lost my brother. I feel like I lost my whole family. God, what a torture his family must have been living with this whole time!

The same painful longing pinches his features. He feels it, too. We lost each other even though we're sitting right here in front of each other.

He recovers first, tries to smile, and leans over to squeeze my hand. "At least we know now. I still feel like you're my sister. Nothing has to change about that."

"Yeah," I breathe. "I really appreciate you being here for me in all of this."

"Of course. Where else would I be?" He nods at the laptop. "You can shut it. We found out what we needed to know."

"Are you okay? I'm sorry it couldn't be different."

"I'm fine. It's okay. I actually...." He smiles at me and then blushes the way he did last night. "I actually feel like I found you after all. I feel like it's okay because I found you. I can't explain it, but I almost feel as good about this as if you were Becca. I still feel the same way about you. Nothing has to change. This doesn't mean anything."

I look down at the report and close the laptop. It's done. We got the answer we needed.

Now we have no choice but to face each other. I feel the same way about Marco. This doesn't change me feeling like he's my brother.

He's been there right next to me all the way. I wouldn't want to go through this without him here.

He even comforts me now—now when he knows I'm just some stranger off the street. He doesn't just walk away and leave me to take the fallout alone.

He squeezes my hand again. "Let's go take a walk. It will take our minds off this. We don't have to do anything. This doesn't mean anything."

He stands up. I have nothing else to do, so I go with him. He takes my hand like we really are brother and sister. I have to transfer my laptop to my other hand so I can hold his.

God, I really wish now that he was my brother! I don't want to lose him. I don't want to lose the way I feel when I'm around him.

He makes me feel like I can never do anything wrong. He makes me feel like I'm the most special person alive. He makes me feel like he would always love me and accept me no matter what else was going on in my life.

I've never felt this way about anyone. I have a brother, but he's younger than I am. I was always the one who took care of him, not the other way around.

That didn't change when we grew up—or I guess it would be more accurate to say that he became independent and didn't need me to take care of him anymore.

He never took care of me. That isn't our relationship.

Marco always takes care of me. He defended me to Angeline. He's the one who should be hurting over this, but he only cares about making sure I'm all right.

We wander into the concourse and start window shopping. He walks slowly so we can see everything. He stops at one of the kids' play zones. We watch kids bouncing on trampolines and climbing the climbing walls.

We wander on until we spot both Donovan and Angeline. They're both in the same restaurant. Donovan sits on a barstool with his arm around a different woman from the one I saw him with the other day.

He's doing something on the bar and then he looks up and kisses her right there in public. Did he ever feel anything for me at all?

Angeline stands across the bar talking to four different guys at once. They all wear business suits. Maybe they're here for a conference or something.

They stand around all smiling at her with the same predatory grin on their faces. She's wearing a tight, scoop-neck halter top and a painted-on skirt that barely comes down to her knees.

The overhead lights glisten on her lustrous blonde curls. She's gorgeous. All these guys can see her for what she is.

Marco and I turn away at the same time. "Hey, do you want to get some lunch?" he asks. "We're already here. We might as well sit down somewhere."

I pull my hand out of his. "I'm not ready to get into a relationship with anyone so soon after breaking up with Donovan. I'm flattered, but I don't feel that way about you."

"Neither do I," he counters. "I meant we would just have lunch together as friends—or as brother and sister—or whatever you want to call it. We just went through something together. We can have lunch together, I think, can't we? I didn't mean it as anything else."

"Okay, sorry." I pass my hand across my eyes. "I don't know where my head is at these days."

"I do. Come on." He takes my hand and leads me to a different restaurant. "Beavis and Butthead aren't here, so we don't have to worry about seeing them again."

I laugh and we both sit down. This is one of the more casual eateries on the ship. It's more of a Denny's-style diner. Everyone in here dresses casually and relaxes while they eat.

I find myself smiling at Marco. "Thanks for understanding. I didn't mean to offend you."

"Of course. "I'm not ready to jump into anything, either. I still need to wrap my head around everything that just happened. The last few days have been a rollercoaster—or maybe something like a marathon. I need a vacation from my vacation."

I laugh again. "Thanks. I'm glad I'm not the only one."

He leans back in his seat and smiles back at me. "I'm really glad I met you. It just doesn't seem to matter anymore if you're Becca or not. I can't explain it any other way, but I actually feel good about this."

"I'm glad you see it that way. I was worried about you after how disappointed you got the first time."

"I was disappointed, but I'm not this time. I'm not sure why because this is so much more decisive a blow. There's no chance we could find out we made a mistake. It's really real this time—but that's okay. I feel like everything is happening for the better. I don't know why because everything that's happening is bad. All of these blows would be enough to kill a person, but I only see them as good. I can't explain it."

"That's so weird!" I exclaim. "I feel the same way. It felt like my breakup with Donovan was a good thing—and then finding out I was adopted didn't really change what started with the breakup."

We have to stop talking when the waitress comes to take our order. We both order something off the breakfast menu even though it's past lunchtime.

Marco leans forward and puts his elbows on the table as soon as she leaves. "I think we should stay in touch after we get back to Wichita Falls. I think you should meet my family."

"Why? I'm not Becca. I can't give them anything they're looking for."

"Maybe you can. You've given me something I'm looking for. I feel better about the whole Becca situation now than I ever have before. I don't want my family to go without that if they could get any relief."

"I don't see how I could give it to them."

"I don't see how you could give it to me, either, but you are. I can't explain why I feel this way. It's almost like finding out that you aren't Becca feels as good if not better than if I found you were Becca." He waves at nothing and looks away. "This whole thing is weird. I don't really know how to deal with any of it."

I touch his arm once. "All right. We can stay in touch when we get back—and I would like to meet your family. It sounds like they all need people who understand why Becca is so important."

"Yes! That's it exactly!" He stares deep into my eyes. "Maybe that's what this is all about—that you understand in ways no one else ever has."

"Have you tried to explain it to people—people other than Angeline?"

"No, that's exactly what I'm saying. It's almost like Becca's disappearance was a curse we all had to carry around with us and not tell anyone. A lot of people found out about it when it happened—obviously—because we came back from vacation with a child missing. And of course all our relatives knew, but no one really understood the darkness inside our family. No one knew it was still going on and on and haunting us year after year and decade after decade. I just got in the habit of not telling anyone so we could all continue to pretend that everything was normal when it wasn't. I guess I did the same thing with Angeline."

"So who's in your family besides you and your parents? What other siblings do you have?"

"Just me and my brother, Wayne. We're the only two besides my parents." He winces. "That's the other thing, you know? I know it's petty and it shouldn't make a difference, but Becca was the apple of my parents' eye. She was their only daughter—and I guess they shared something with her that they couldn't share with me and Wayne."

"It isn't petty at all. Of course they would have a different relationship with her. Mothers and fathers always have different relationships with their daughters as they do with their sons."

He stares at me again like he has trouble believing I can be so understanding of his situation.

He shudders before he goes on. "Anyway, they lost something when they lost her. My mom was never going to have another daughter and neither was my dad. They lost the whole dream of her being their little girl, watching her grow up, my dad walking her down the aisle—all that stuff. Wayne and I lost that, too, you know? She was our little sister. I got all protective of her when she started school. I kept telling her to let me know if anyone messed with her. I took the whole big-brother role super seriously—and Wayne did, too. No one was gonna mess with our little sister or there would be Hell to pay."

I burst into a grin. "That is so sweet."

"Anyway, I don't want to talk about that."

I find myself gripping his hand again. "I'm honored that you think of me that way. I've never had that from anyone."

"What about you? What siblings do you have?"

"I have an older sister and a younger brother. I got a letter from my mom after they told me about the adoption. She said she tried to get pregnant for two years after they had my sister. They thought they were infertile. That's why they adopted me—and then two years later they randomly got pregnant with my brother. He never acted protective of me. I was always the big sister showing him what to do."

"That's sad. Every girl needs a big brother."

I can't help but beam at him. "Well, now I have one."

Chapter 13: Marco

I lean against the railing in the ship's prow and turn my face into the breeze. This is my favorite spot to come and think.

Couples come out here to spend romantic time together, but no one is here now. I have the place to myself.

Jenn isn't Becca, but she's just as special to me now as she was just a few hours ago before I found out the truth.

I feel better, now that I know she isn't Becca. I feel better than if I did find out she was Becca.

I don't understand myself or anything else about this situation. I only know I have to keep Jenn in my life. She's too important.

It's almost like some higher power sent her on this cruise so she could be here for me and give me this priceless gift. I could never push that away.

Thank all the stars in heaven she lives in the same city I do. I'll be able to keep in touch with her and introduce her to my family. I don't know if anything will come of that, but I have to try.

The wind gets cooler as the sun goes down. I should go inside. I should come up with some plan of what I'm going to do tonight, but

I can only think about spending time with Jenn. Nothing else seems as important as that.

We're meeting up later to talk. I can't get enough of talking to her. Her presence makes me want to pour out my soul and all my most closely guarded secrets. That's how I know this is right.

I don't know what's right about it. I don't know if I want to pursue a relationship with her. I'm not ready for a relationship right now anyway.

I don't even care about pursuing a relationship with her. Just talking to her, sharing our thoughts, and getting to know her feels like more than enough right now—so technically we are pursuing a relationship. It's just a platonic one.

I don't want to turn away from the ocean. It's so beautiful at this time of day. It could only get better if Jenn was here.

I'm standing there daydreaming about how special she is when Angeline comes up to my side. All my good feeling goes up in smoke the minute I lay eyes on her.

"You're having a good time, aren't you," I snarl.

"Can't we work things out, Marco?" she asks. "I'm sorry I flew off the handle the way I did."

"You did a lot more than fly off the handle," I mutter.

"What do you want me to do—go down on bended knee?" Tears spring to her eyes. "Just give me another chance."

I lean forward and pronounce the next word extra loudly and clearly. "NO! Do you understand that by now? The answer....is no. I don't know how I can get it through your head. I will never give you another chance. There are some things that you only get one chance at. You said you would back me up in everything. You said you would always have my back and support me through thick and thin. You didn't. You can't. You're incapable of it—and now you're out there sleeping with half the ship."

"I am not!" Tears streak down her cheeks. "How can you be so cruel?!"

"You called my sister make-believe! You called her a bitch. You called her a skank and a whore and then you called her a liar when you were the one out there sleeping around. Do you think I could ever forgive that? Don't start turning on the waterworks to manipulate me into taking you back. You're a great actress, you know that? Go cry to one of your playmates down in the bar. I'm sure they would love to buy you a few drinks and take your mind off it. You got busted for being the selfish tramp that you are. You got exactly what you deserved."

"Please, Marco!" She chokes on her own tears. "I'm at the end of my rope."

"Good. Maybe you'll think about your actions from now on." I turn away from her. "Troy warned you to leave me alone. Get out of here. I never want to see you again."

She lets out a few more racking sobs. Her makeup smears and her whole face and body heaves with misery, but I don't fall for it. She's trying to mess with me again.

I would never let her close enough to me to hurt Jenn again. Jenn is going to be in my life for a long, long time if I have anything to say about it.

I can never let Angeline back in—not if there is any chance she could hurt Jenn.

Angeline *would* hurt Jenn again. Angeline would make side remarks or, if she didn't, there would always be an underlying current of resentment between them.

And that's saying nothing about what she did to me. Some crimes are unforgivable. I crossed a line with her. I won't go back.

She turns away from me, too. I expect her to run back inside the ship, but she turns the other way—toward the prow.

Before I can even think to realize what she's doing, she steps up on the rail and throws herself off into the water right underneath the prow.

I yell out, "No—Angeline!" but it's too late. She vanishes under the water and then the boat plows right over that spot.

I charge back toward the piazza to sound the emergency stop alarm. Then I remember there's another emergency stop button next to the pool.

I smash down the button and a deafening alarm goes off all over the boat. The engines cut out and the boat comes to a stop.

I race back to the prow and look over. I don't see Angeline anywhere. I look on both sides of the boat, but she isn't there, either. I only pray to God she didn't go all the way under the ship.

The alarm triggers a stampede among the other passengers. Everyone goes nuts and people flood out on deck trying to figure out what happened.

The ship must have some kind of system that tells the staff and crew which alarm got pressed. Troy and the security team shows up a second later.

"She jumped off the prow!" I can barely breathe well enough to speak. "She jumped off the prow! She went down....right there!"

The security guys look over the side in all directions, too. My stomach drops into my shoes the longer this goes on. Angeline would have surfaced by now if she was going to surface at all.

Troy takes hold of my sleeve and pulls me back inside the piazza. "You come with me." He escorts me to his office and parks me in a chair. "The dive rescue team is on its way out on deck right now.

They'll go down and look for her. You stay here until they decide what's what. Okay? Don't go back out there."

I nod in a shocked stupor. I can't think. Angeline did not just throw herself off the prow of a moving cruise ship. Why on Earth would she do that?

She was the one who broke up with me. She was the one who said we wouldn't have a relationship if I talked to or even looked at Jenn.

How can Angeline get so overwrought and hopeless over a breakup she caused? I never would have broken up with her if not for this. She did all of this.

She must have been out of her mind if she threw herself off the boat. She couldn't have been thinking clearly. She had her whole life ahead of her. I hope she still does.

My shock turns to agitation when I hear banging outside. I stand up planning to pace Troy's office until he comes to tell me something.

Pacing brings me closer to the windows. I shouldn't look, but I wind up seeing a diver in full scuba gear surfacing right at that moment.

The captain and some of the senior officers line the ship's rail. They lean over to call out to the diver. He calls back as he swims toward a rope ladder they throw down for him to climb up. I can't hear what any of them are saying.

They must have cleared all the passengers off the deck. I don't see any other people out there—just members of the crew, the security guys, a bunch of medical people, and the dive team.

The diver grabs the ladder and starts climbing. I'm just about to turn away from the window when three other divers surface on that side of the boat. They all wear black wetsuits, masks, and scuba gear.

They bring something white to the surface with them. The white is Angeline's blouse and skirt. Her hair trails in the water. She's floating on her stomach with her face buried in the ocean.

I get a sick feeling in my stomach when the divers roll her onto her back. Her hair plasters across her face. Her wet clothes stick to her body.

She doesn't open her eyes. She doesn't splutter or flounder or cough the water out of her mouth. She doesn't move at all.

The crewmen on deck lower an emergency medical backboard on a winch. The divers float Angeline onto the board, strap her down, and the crew winches her back on deck. She doesn't open her eyes the whole time.

The medical team surrounds her. They start doing CPR right away and then the doctor hooks her up to a defibrillator. The medical team moves back while the doctor takes some readings on Angeline's heart.

The medical team doesn't start working on her again. They leave her there.

The crew starts packing up and putting all their equipment away. The medical people disconnect the electrodes from Angeline's chest. The divers climb up to the deck and take off their equipment.

Angeline's body lies there without moving. I can't see what killed her.

I killed her. I pushed her away when she was too upset. I shouldn't have treated her so harshly. I could have shown her some compassion even though I didn't plan to take her back.

I sink back down in the chair and stare at my hands. She's dead—because of me. How did this happen?

I called her a selfish tramp, but I'm the one who is selfish. I didn't have to twist the knife like that. I didn't have to take out my pain on her.

I could have turned her down more politely. I could have done a lot of things to soften the blow. I was selfish not to.

Troy comes back, but he doesn't talk to me or even come near me—not right away. He studies me from across the room and then leaves again.

He leaves me sitting there in silence for what seems like hours. The sun goes down and the office falls into darkness before he comes back a second time.

He switches on a lamp over his desk. It casts a soft, golden light over the office without being too harsh or disturbing the ghost-like atmosphere. I need that right now.

He comes over to me, rests his hand on my shoulder, and sits down in the chair next to me. "Go upstairs to your cabin," he murmurs low. "You can't do anything here. Come on. You can't stay here."

He grasps my elbow and steers me to my feet. I follow blindly. I don't know what's happening to me or even who I am anymore. Angeline is dead because of me.

He takes me into the elevator and up to my cabin. He uses his own key to open the door. He must have key code access to every cabin on the ship. That makes sense. He would need to break in if there was any kind of emergency in someone's cabin.

He leads me inside, switches on another lamp, sits me down on the couch, squeezes my shoulder one more time, and leaves.

I stare into space for what seems like hours. I can't even think except that Angeline is dead because of me.

I look down at my hands. I might as well have thrown her off the prow with my own hands. Now she's dead. What will I ever tell her family when I get back home?

Chapter 14: Jenn

A bunch of people stand around in groups in the *Electric Emerald's* main concourse. They talk in low, worried tones.

They're all talking about the woman who killed herself by throwing herself off the ship's prow—or did she? No one knows anything except that the security team is still investigating her death.

The medical team already choppered her body off the ship. Her body is on its way back to the States for a full autopsy. No one will rule on her cause of death until the ship's security team finishes its investigation.

I wander through the concourse, but the atmosphere of tension and anxiety doesn't ease. No one can relax or enjoy themselves with this hanging over the ship.

I stop in front of one of the jewelry stores. Nothing in the window appeals to me.

I don't have to think too hard about what happened. I haven't seen Marco or Angeline since the incident. The person who fell over the side was a woman. That means Angeline is the one who died.

Marco mentioned after our lunch date that she wanted to get him back and he turned her down. Did she throw herself off the boat in a suicide bid to make him pity her—or something?

I don't want to think about this. It has nothing to do with me. I'm planning to go outside to the pool when Troy Nixon comes walking down the concourse. He comes out of one of the restaurants on his usual round of checking in with all the staff.

Other passengers mob him the minute he shows up. "What's happening with the investigation?" one woman asks him.

"I can't tell you that," he replies. "It's confidential until we come to some conclusion. You should all go back to your normal activities."

"Can't you tell us anything?" a man asks. "How can we not worry about it when there could be a cold-blooded killer on the loose?"

More people gather around and chime in with questions and demands to know what's going on.

Troy eventually sighs. "There is no cold-blooded killer on the loose. The woman's death was definitely suicide. We got the whole thing on security camera footage. The man who was with her at the time never laid a finger on her. We have clear footage of her climbing onto the rail and jumping off. The guy was in the act of walking away from her at the time. You have nothing to worry about. The woman's body isn't even on the ship anymore. You have no reason not to go on with the cruise and enjoy yourselves. The investigation is concluding now. It's all over and done with."

Murmurs of relief and speculation run through the crowd. "Did he say something to make her jump?" another woman asks. "Are you investigating the guy?"

Troy's tone and expression change instantly. "There is nothing anyone could have said to make a grown woman jump off the boat. It's obvious from the whole interaction that she planned this ahead of time. She jumped off right at the point of the prow—right where she would get sucked under the ship at its longest point—right where she would most likely either get crushed by the ship driving over her or where she would get pulled into the propellors. She planned to kill herself. That's all you need to know."

He walks off and leaves people still exchanging bits of gossip and wild conjecture. Then everyone breaks up and goes back to what they were doing.

Troy has to stop and talk to a dozen more clusters of people before he leaves the concourse. The atmosphere lightens more and more the farther he goes. No one has to speculate or guess anymore.

I turn away and head for the elevator. Poor Marco. He must be devastated over this. I wouldn't be surprised if he blames himself for Angeline's death. She tried to get him back. He turned her down. Then this happened.

I want to talk to him and assure him that it isn't his fault, but I can't even find him. I search the ship from stem to stern. I even knock on his cabin door, but I don't get any response.

"Marco—are you in there?!" I yell through the door. "It's me—Jenn! Let's just talk about this! You don't have to go through this alone!"

I don't get any response, so I go back to searching. I cross every deck and stick my nose into every activity, restaurant, theater, and showroom. I don't find Marco anywhere.

I'm just on my way out to the pools for the fifth time when Donovan comes around the corner. He stops in his tracks when he sees me.

I stiffen expecting him to give me the silent treatment, but he comes up to me instead. "Do you mind if we sit down somewhere and talk?" he asks.

He says it in a quiet undertone—like he used to.

I open my mouth to tell him where to shove it, but I change my mind when I remember Angeline.

"Okay," I tell him. "We can sit and talk."

We head down the piazza and wind up going out to the rear deck. It's deserted as usual.

Marco takes my hand and squeezes it. "I missed you," he begins.

I pull my hand out of his grasp. "I didn't miss you. If you came over here expecting to make up with me, you're sadly mistaken. We are NOT getting back together."

"Just hear me out," he insists. "This whole suicide thing—it's making me realize what we had."

I look away. I want to read him the riot act, but Angeline's death makes me hesitate.

Marco probably read Angeline the riot act—just like he did in their cabin. He had every right to read her the riot act. I can't fault him for that.

Donovan takes my hand again. "I messed up, okay?" he murmurs. "I know that. I shouldn't have made a big deal about you finding out if that guy was your cousin...."

"That guy is Troy Nixon." I try to keep the ice out of my voice. "He's the Security Chief for the whole ship. I never hit on him and he never hit on me. You acted like a child."

"I know," he breathes. "And I'm sorry."

"Did you apologize to him? Did you tell him you know he didn't do anything? Did you tell him you know you acted like a child?"

"That isn't important. I want to talk about us. I want to work this out so we can get back together. We had a good thing. Don't throw that away."

I don't tell him he was the one who threw it away. I don't tell him we will never get back together.

"We came on this cruise to get serious about each other," he goes on. "Let's just get back to that—to you and me. Forget all this other stuff."

"Let me ask you one question," I tell him. "How many women have you slept with on this cruise since you moved out of the cabin?"

He cringes and looks away again. That answers my question—like I really needed to ask.

I pull my hand away. "I don't want to get back together. Things have changed for me since you dumped me....."

"I didn't dump you. I just....I needed to straighten a few things out in my own mind."

"You needed to straighten them out by sleeping with other people? We crossed a line and we can't un-cross it. It's too late, Donovan. What we had is gone. We can never get it back. I'm sorry. We won't get back together."

His voice trembles and his features spasm. "Isn't there any chance?"

"No, there isn't. I'm sorry. You ended our relationship. There is nothing to get back. If you really understand that you messed up, maybe you'll take steps to make sure it doesn't happen in your next relationship. That's the best I can do for you. I hope you work this out for yourself. It will just keep ruining more relationships for you in the future if you don't work it out. I'm sorry. I gotta go."

I stand up to leave, but he grabs my hand. "Don't walk away from me, Jenn. I love you. I've never loved anyone the way I love you. I can't live without you. I don't know what I'll do if you don't give me another chance."

I lose my patience with him and snap, "You better never let anyone hear you talking like that again. A lot of people on this ship are upset about that woman killing herself. People might get the idea to lock you up for your own safety."

I yank my hand out of his grasp and hurry away before he can say anything else. I have to fight myself every minute not to lay into him with all my fury.

What is he thinking? How can he not realize how badly he screwed up? He wouldn't come crawling back expecting me to forgive him if he did realize.

He doesn't think apologizing to Troy is important. Donovan thinks we can just go back to acting romantic toward each other like none of this ever happened.

I race up to my cabin and shut myself in. I can't stop shaking with fury. I need to get all of this out somehow—without driving another person to suicide.

I shut my cabin door, go into my bedroom, and shut that door, too, before I lie down on my bed.

I turn on my stomach, bury my face in the pillow, and bellow all my rage, pain, and frustration into the pillow where no one will be able to hear me.

I have to let it out. I have to express it somehow. I can't risk letting it out on Donovan or any other living person. I don't trust myself not to do something terrible if I did.

Chapter 15: Marco

Troy Nixon stands up from behind his desk when I walk into his office. He holds out his hand to shake mine. "Thank you for coming in," he tells me. "Take a seat."

I say, "Yes, Sir," and sit down. He's been acting so close and caring toward me. I probably don't have to use all this formal protocol with him, but it seems especially fitting right now of all times.

He doesn't tell me again that I don't have to use it. Maybe he gets it that I have to.

I'm getting called into his office on official business. Using this protocol matters now more than ever.

He leans back in his seat and holds up his phone. "I'm going to record your statement for the official investigation report. The computer system will transcribe it into text. Is that okay with you?"

"Yes, Sir," I reply.

He taps the phone screen, puts the phone in front of me, and says, "So tell me what happened from the very beginning. Don't leave anything out."

I take a deep breath. "When Angeline and I first checked in on the boat, we showed up for the safety briefing like everyone else."

"Uh-huh," he replies. "I remember seeing you there. You guys looked like you were having an argument or something."

"I spotted a woman in the crowd who looked like my sister. My sister vanished in a boating accident in Florida when she was six years old. No one ever found her body and my parents spent twenty-five years searching for her. It tore my family apart and my parents had computer-generated renderings of my sister created so we would be able to tell what she looked like after she grew up. This woman looked exactly like the renderings. Angeline completely lost the plot when she saw me staring at this woman. Angeline refused to let me go near the woman even to find out if she was my sister. We had a few heated exchanges and I told her I was going to find out one way or the other. She wouldn't back down and she threw me out of the bedroom to go spend the night in the other room on our very night on board the ship."

Troy raises his eyebrows. "That's pretty harsh."

"That's what I said. She flatly refused to support me or to believe that I wasn't trying to hit on this woman. I bumped into the woman a few times and tried to talk to her, but she thought I was hitting on her, too. I finally got a chance to explain it to her and we talked. She explained that she had never been to Florida in her life, so we figured she couldn't possibly be my sister. I went back to the cabin and got into another argument with Angeline because she saw me talking to this woman in what Angeline assumed was a romantic way."

"Was it romantic?" Troy asks.

"NO! Not at all! You can ask her. She'll tell you."

"Who? Who would tell me?"

"Jenn. Jenn Hayworth."

Now he really raises his eyebrows. "Jenn Hayworth is the woman you thought was your sister?"

"Yes! She knows all about this."

"Okay. Go on. So what happened? You got in a fight with Angeline because she saw you talking to Jenn and assumed it was romantic."

"Angeline stormed out—like as in she actually moved out of the cabin and said we were over. I checked with the purser to remove her name from the booking agreement and I changed the locks so she couldn't come back."

"That was a little harsh, wasn't it?"

"What makes you say that? She kicked me in the face just for trying to find out if Jenn was my sister. Angeline got completely, irrationally jealous just from me looking at Jenn."

"Was that the first time you ever looked at another woman?"

"Yes! I never gave her any reason to doubt me before. She was all affectionate and ready for me to propose to her just a few minutes before this. She wouldn't even listen when I explained the story about my sister."

His eyes go hard. "So you never told her about your sister before? Why not?"

I take a deep breath and cover my eyes. "It's a long story. Losing my sister wrecked our family. It took a long time for any of us to get back to something like normal—or maybe we never got completely back to normal. I guess that's what I was trying to do—get back to normal, move on, and put it behind me. We all looked for her and hoped for the best for so long and never had any luck. It just seemed like it might be time to forget all about it. I never thought we would ever find her."

"So you found out Jenn wasn't your sister. Then what?"

"I had already made up my mind to split up with Angeline even before she moved out. I just want to make that clear. Her behavior was so selfish and irrational that I decided I couldn't propose to her or even stay with her. She accused me of making up the whole story about my sister so I could stare at another woman when I never looked sideways at another woman the whole time we were together! I was planning to break it off. I just thought I better wait a while until I got my head clear and I wasn't so disappointed over finding out the truth about Jenn."

He nods. "Okay. So what happened then?"

"Angeline tried to make up with me like none of it ever happened. She came back to the cabin and tried to cozy up to me. I went out by myself for a while because I still needed to think about everything. She stayed in the room. When I came back she was gone. I was there by myself when Jenn showed up all agitated and upset. She said she mentioned me to her parents and they dropped a bomb by telling her that she was adopted. She never knew. The circumstances made it seem like she could be my sister after all and her parents agreed to send out the adoption paperwork for us to look at. We were sitting there talking when Angeline came back, saw Jenn, completely flew off the handle, called Jenn a skank and a whore and a bitch, and Jenn ran off. Angeline and I went at it again and I told her it was completely over and I would never get back together with her. I told her not to come near me again and, if she did, I would have security remove her from my cabin. That's when I had the conversation with you about the same thing—and then later, Jenn spotted Angeline hooking up with that guy in the broom closet—which she lied about and tried to make it out that Jenn was conning me by making up the whole story. I saw Angeline flirting with other guys in public plenty of times after that."

"Okay. So did Jenn turn out to be your sister after all?"

"No, we got the adoption paperwork and it turned out she was adopted from a different part of the country. She couldn't be my sister, but we still felt attached to each other as if we were. We went out to lunch, and afterward, I went out to the prow to think things over. That's when Angeline showed up and it all went down from there."

"So what happened when she met you at the prow? The footage shows you talking to each other. That's all we know."

I look down at my hands. "I guess you could say I was overly harsh with her then, too. I'm not proud of it."

"What did you say to her?"

"Nothing you can't imagine," I mumble. "I basically just repeated all the things she did to me and to Jenn—and her sleeping around. I told her again that there was no chance I would ever get back together with her—but I didn't try to be diplomatic about it. I wanted to hurt her and I did."

"You aren't to blame for her death. You want to be clear about your intention to break up with her. Let me be clear about this. You are not responsible for your death. From what you just told me, it sounds like she wanted to get your attention by doing something drastic. Maybe she wanted you to believe she was suicidal when she actually wasn't. I don't think she realized how dangerous it would be to jump off the prow right at that point."

"Of course she knew," I mutter under my breath. "That's exactly why she did it—because she knew how dangerous it was."

"Then you must also know that whatever you said to her couldn't possibly drive her to suicide just in a few short days. You say she was affectionate and loving when you boarded the ship."

I nod. "Everything was perfect before I saw Jenn."

"Then that proves my point. She started all of this by being irrational and self-centered. You had every right to break up with her."

"I didn't have every right to be deliberately cruel to her."

"Then she had no right to say you made up the story and to call Jenn a bunch of nasty names when she wasn't even involved in any of this."

He leans forward, taps his phone to turn off the voice recorder, stands up, and puts the phone in his pocket.

"Come downstairs with me," he tells me. "We're going to talk to Dr. McKinlay about his preliminary examination of the body."

"What will that accomplish?"

"Just come on. I have your statement. I want you to hear his assessment of the situation."

Chapter 16: Marco

I have nothing better to do with my life, so I stand up and follow Troy out of his office and down the corridor to the elevator. A different elevator goes down into the lower decks of the ship.

The staff and crew use that elevator to bring supplies and stuff up from the storage and utility areas of the ship. They don't want to interfere with passengers riding up and down from their cabins.

The utility elevator goes all the way down into the hold. Troy and I get out in an industrial or maybe institutional style corridor with stark fluorescent lights, hospital floor tiles, and absolutely zero decoration or amenities.

He leads me into the ship's infirmary. This is the first time I've ever been down here. I really hope it's the last.

We meet up with a young doctor with the name, *Dr. Cameron McKinley, Emergency Medicine*, embroidered on his lab coat. Troy introduces me.

"This is Angeline Harvey's boyfriend, Marco de Rossi," Troy tells him. "This is Dr. McKinlay. He's our senior medical director on board the ship."

I nod at Dr. McKinlay. He's a lot younger than I expected. "Good to meet you," I tell him.

"I'm sorry for your loss. Troy tells me you wanted to find out about my preliminary findings from examining the body."

"I....I guess so."

He grabs his tablet from the workbench on the side of the room and scrolls on the screen. "She was killed by blunt force trauma to her head when the ship drove over her. She would have been killed within seconds of hitting the water. The examination shows that she stopped breathing before any water entered her lungs."

I glare at him. "Is that supposed to make me feel better?"

"The toxicology report indicates she had a blood alcohol concentration of 2.5 percent—more than four times the legal limit. According to the law, she would not be considered competent to make decisions for herself, operate a vehicle, or enter a plea in court." He looks up from his device. "Does that make you feel better?"

I stagger backward and my hand flies to my head. "Oh, my God!"

"Did you notice her acting altered?" Troy asks.

"No! She was acting normal—as normal as she ever did."

"Initial examination of her organs revealed swelling and the early stages of cirrhosis in her liver," Dr. McKinlay goes on. "She had a severe alcohol problem long before she ever came on board the ship."

My jaw drops. I can't even make a sound. Angeline did not have an alcohol problem—unless she hid it from me. Is that even possible? Could she have hidden it so well that I didn't notice any difference?

If she appeared to be acting normally right before she jumped—but she had a blood alcohol level that high—then I wouldn't have noticed her acting any differently any other time.

Troy and Dr. McKinley exchange glances. I read volumes in that glance. They talked about this before. They talked about bringing me down here and breaking the news like this so they could see my reaction.

I turn away and my knees wobble when I try to take a step. They both grab me and steer me into some seats against the wall. Then they both sit down on either side of me.

"I'm going to assume from your reaction that you never knew," Troy remarks.

"A lot of hardcore, chronic alcoholics get very good at hiding their addiction," Dr. McKinlay goes on. "You shouldn't blame yourself for not noticing—and no one could have prevented her death."

"You couldn't have prevented it even if you treated her kindly or even if you took her back," Troy adds. "She was out of her mind drunk."

My hand flies to my head again. "I can't believe it! I mean...seriously?! It can't be!"

"Does it help to explain her irrational, erratic behavior?" Troy asks.

"I can't deal with this! I gotta get out of here!" I stand up and waver a second before I catch my balance. Neither of them stands up. "Are you done with me? Can I go?"

"Yeah, sure," Troy tells me. "Just....take care of yourself, okay—and don't do anything crazy."

I mumble, "I won't," and stagger out of the infirmary.

I get into the elevator and ride back up to the piazza. Angeline....a secret alcoholic.....

How else can I explain her suddenly turning on me for no reason? Troy is right. It does explain her behavior—at least some of it.

I stumble around the piazza trying to decide what to do with myself—and with all this information in my head.

What if Troy and Dr. McKinlay are right that I'm not responsible for Angeline's death? Could they be right about that, too?

The blood alcohol concentration at the time of her death staggers my mind. I can hardly comprehend how someone could be walking around with that much alcohol in their system and still be functioning.

She must have had an unbelievable tolerance built up over years. Her liver was developing cirrhosis. Jesus Christ! She must have been so far gone.

She might not have jumped overboard. She could have stumbled in front of a moving truck—or fallen overboard—or fallen into the pool. She could have died any of a thousand ways with a blood alcohol concentration that high.

I've never gone over the legal limit in my life. I find it hard to believe anyone could or would actually drink that much—but I guess addiction will do that to you.

How can I not have known? How did she hide it from me for so long?

I never smelled it on her breath. I never smelled it on her clothes. She would have had to be a true professional to pull that one off.

It does explain some of her behavior—like lying about getting caught sleeping around—and blaming Jenn for being a con artist.

Angeline might have been tanked when she hooked up with that guy. She might not even have remembered hooking up with him. Maybe that's why she denied it and then immediately regretted it when I showed her the footage.

How many other guys has she hooked up with while she and I were together? It could be a lot if she was that gone.

I lean against the piazza windows trying to get my head screwed on straight. How am I supposed to process this?

I must never have known the real Angeline. I went out with the bottle. I talked to the bottle. I lived with it. I was even planning to propose to it.

The real Angeline never entered our relationship. I never even met her. She probably went underground decades ago and never resurfaced.

Now what am I supposed to do with this information? Should I just keep it to myself? I don't know if I can do that. I need to talk to someone about this—but who?

Someone touches my shoulder just then. I jolt out of my trance, spin around, and wilt when I see Jenn at my side.

"Hey! I've been looking all over for you." She frowns at me. "Are you okay? I don't even know why I ask. Of course you're not. Do you want to take a walk and talk about it?"

I look away. I was just thinking I needed to talk about this. Now the most perfect person is here.

I don't want to talk to Jenn about Angeline. I don't want to spoil my time with Jenn by dragging up all that negativity.

She doesn't wait for me to answer. She tugs my sleeve and says, "Come on."

I blunder after her. Now I'm the one completely out of my mind. My brain doesn't want to kick into gear.

We wander around some of the decks, some of the concourse, some of the activity levels, and wind up back in the breezeway.

She glances toward the pools. "You probably don't want to go over there. Let's go to one of the observation lounges."

She sticks me in an elevator. At least someone around here can still function like a responsible adult.

She sits me on the couch in the lounge, sits down next to me, and rubs my back just like we really are brother and sister.

"Troy told us all that Angeline's death was ruled a suicide," she tells me.

I nod. "It was a little more than that."

She turns around to stare at me. "What do you mean?"

I open my mouth. Should I tell her?

She reads my mind. "You don't have to tell me anything. I know it's private."

"It isn't that. I want to tell you. I just don't know if I should."

"You don't have to. No one is going to make you, but maybe talking about it will make you feel better."

"I'm sure it will make me feel better. It will probably make you feel worse."

"Maybe you won't blame yourself for her death if you talk about it," she tells me.

"I don't blame myself for her death. I did, but I don't anymore."

"Did something happen to change your mind? You looked distressed downstairs."

I snort and cover my face with both hands. I really need to talk to her, but I still hold back.

This turmoil is eating me up inside. I can't keep holding it in.

She touches my shoulder again. "Do you want me to leave you alone?" she murmurs. "Maybe you just need to take some time to clear your head."

"No! Don't leave." I take my hands down, but I still can't look at her. "I just had an interview and gave a statement with Troy—about everything. He knows everything—about you, me, Becca—all of it."

"He doesn't hold you responsible, does he? He was the one going around the ship telling everyone you *weren't* responsible."

"It isn't that. He took me downstairs to meet Dr. McKinlay. He's the senior doctor on board. He had to do a preliminary examination on Angeline before they sent her body back to the States for a full autopsy."

Her face drains of all color. "What did he find?"

I look up at her. I can't look away once I make eye contact with her. I have to tell her. I can't let her think this is about her—or us.

"She had a blood alcohol concentration of 2.5 percent," I blurt out. "She was off her skull drunk—and she had been completely tanked for years. She was a hardcore alcoholic through our whole relationship—and she kept it hidden from me. They found the early stages of cirrhosis in her liver. She was blotto. She was out of her gourd. She had no idea what she was doing or saying or who she was banging or what she was lying about or anything—for the whole of our relationship! She was totally impaired when she jumped off the prow—like certifiably mentally incompetent."

Jenn gasps and her mouth and eyes fall open when she stares at me. "No way!" she whispers.

I nod. "She was obliterated."

"Oh, my God!" she breathes. "I had no idea!"

"Neither did I. Dr. McKinlay says hardcore alcoholics get really good at hiding it—and she was—but it explains so much, doesn't it? She was jealously paranoid—and irrational—and sleeping with random guys....Maybe she didn't even remember sleeping with that guy. Maybe that's why she denied it—and then regretted it when she saw the footage....." I trail off and cover my eyes. "I need to stop thinking about this. It's driving me crazy."

She squeezes my hand. "Come downstairs and let's go have dinner somewhere. It won't be a date or anything. It will just be to take your mind off it and so you don't have to be alone with all of this. Come on."

She tugs me back to my feet and she doesn't let go of my hand this time. She leads me to the elevator and we both get in.

"I should be taking you out to dinner," I remark on the way down.

She smiles at me. "You're the best company on this ship. Trust me."

I turn to look down at her. "I feel the same way about you. I hope you don't think I was avoiding you."

"It's fine if you were. You had a lot to deal with. You still do. I understood why you wanted to be alone. I would have, too, if that happened to me."

I look away. "Thanks. I knew you would understand."

"Of course I do." She squeezes my hand again. "No sane person would want to go through the ordeal you're going through right now. It's a nightmare."

Chapter 17: Jenn

I step out of the elevator in the piazza and lead Marco to the concourse. The usual number of passengers and staff bustle everywhere. The place throbs with noise.

It's five o'clock in the afternoon, so the concourse is just starting to heat up with the dinnertime crowds and people coming to see shows and enjoy the nightlife.

I take Marco to one of the nicer restaurants. We aren't dressed for a date. We both wear casual clothes, but who cares?

He starts to come back to his senses when we get a table for two and sit down. "Thank you for doing this," he tells me. "I really needed this."

"You bet. I'll do whatever I can to get you through this."

"You're always so understanding."

"I mean—Jesus! You need a friend after everything that's been happening—and now this! It's enough to make anyone's head spin."

"I know, right? I almost fell over when the doctor told me about the alcohol use."

"And you never saw a sign? That's amazing. She must have been a real pro."

"That's what I said. She never acted paranoid or irrational before. I never saw her having a problem driving or anything like that. She was always really competent at everything."

"Maybe her addiction just hadn't come to a tipping point yet, you know? Maybe she could still manage it well enough."

He shakes his head down at his plate. "I don't think I'll ever understand it."

I grip his arm just above the wrist. "Don't start blaming yourself for that, too. It isn't your fault."

"I'm not blaming myself. That's the one thing the doctor did accomplish. He finally got it through my head that I couldn't have saved her even if I knew. I couldn't have saved her by being nice to her and softening the blow when I said I wouldn't take her back. Something would have happened. She would have made a mistake somewhere along the line and gotten herself killed. It just turned out to be that the alcohol made her do something irrationally stupid. Troy thinks she made a suicide play to get me to pity her. He doesn't think she planned to kill herself."

Jenn shrugs. "I suppose that makes sense if she was that far gone. She planned it a little too well, didn't she?"

The waitress comes and takes our order just then.

"I don't want to talk about Angeline anymore," he tells me after she leaves.

"What would you like to talk about?"

"I want to talk about you. I don't know anything about you. What do you even do for a living?"

"I'm a high school music teacher."

Now he's the one whose jaw drops. "No flippin' way!"

I laugh. "It's a great job. I love it."

"Aren't the kids....like.....hooligans?"

I can't stop laughing. "They might be outside the classroom. They're all super enthusiastic about music when they get into my class. They can't get enough of it—and they're really creative and really motivated. They're the best. I love them, too. It's wonderful to see them develop and to be part of giving them the inspiration to be the best they can be."

He stares at me in awe. "That is amazing. I never would have guessed that."

"What did you think—that I was some accountant's secretary?"

"Yeah, something like that."

"What do you do?" I ask.

"I'm a life coach and counselor in the prison. I counsel and coach the prisoners on how to get their lives together so they don't get locked up again."

Now I'm the one gaping at him with my mouth open. "That's incredible!"

"It's a wonderful job. I love it. I look forward to every single day. It's like you said. I love watching them develop new confidence in themselves, grapple with their mental blocks, and overcoming them to build new, empowered lives."

"Wow," I breathe. "I never would have guessed that."

Now it's his turn to laugh. He's coming back more and more with every passing second. "What did you think I was?"

"I thought you were a doctor or something like that. I thought you were some kind of administrator or maybe a professor or something."

"Yuck!" he exclaims. "I couldn't spend my life in an office."

"But...you do have an office, don't you?"

"Yeah...but that isn't the point! It isn't that kind of office."

I laugh and the waitress comes over just then with our orders.

"So tell me how you became a teacher," Marco prompts when we start eating.

"I guess you could say I got inspired by the teachers I had growing up. They were all really kind and patient with me. I didn't know it at the time, but I realize now that my parents must have told the teachers and all the school administrators that I was recovering from a head injury. I just thought everyone was really nice. They helped me a lot—and I needed it."

"Why music?" he asks. "Was there a music teacher who meant a lot to you?"

"The music teacher I had was nothing special. He just did his job, but I always loved music. Music really helped me, too. Sometimes it was the only subject I could even understand. I wanted to make music my life, but I didn't want to become a professional musician and do the whole touring, gigging, and band practice thing. I wanted to help kids who might be having the same problems I had—or any other kind of problems. So I combined the two into this. What about you? What made you go into prison work."

He studies me for a second. "I'm not sure if I should tell you."

"Why? Are you a government agent or something?"

"It isn't that. It's....." He breaks off again. "Okay. I'm going to tell you because I have a really good feeling about you."

"Why the hesitation? What's the big secret?"

"Do you remember when we talked about you meeting my family—even though you aren't Becca?"

"I don't have to. I have no reason to meet them—unless you want me to."

"I don't know why, but I have a strong gut feeling that you will meet them. I'm not sure how or if it will have anything to do with the whole Becca thing. Just call it a gut feeling."

"Okay, but what does that have to do with your career?"

"I'm going to tell you, but I'm trusting you to treat this as sensitive personal information. I have a really good feeling about you and I know you're a good person who wouldn't hold this over anyone's head or treat them badly because of it."

I gape at him. "What on Earth are you talking about?! Why would I hold it over anyone's head?"

"My brother Wayne got arrested and sent to prison when he was young. He's two years older than I am the whole Becca thing affected him in a different way. He went a little crazy—lost control of his temper for a while—pulled a few robberies—got into a few assaults—stole some cars—and got himself sent to prison. That's what I mean about holding it over him. You would have to treat it sensitively if you ever met him in person—which I'm certain you will. He's fine now. He pulled his life together. He's married with a beautiful wife and two gorgeous children. He has a good job and he's a productive member of society. Hardly anyone knows he served time and we all want to keep it that way."

I slump in my chair and blink at him. "Oh. I understand now. That sounds really hard on him."

"Anyway, that's why I decided to do this work. I felt like he got a raw deal. He wound up in prison when what he really needed was therapy to deal with all the issues surrounding Becca's disappearance. I figured a lot of guys who wind up in prison are in the same boat. They got caught in bad home life situations that could have been resolved another way—some way that would have kept them out of prison entirely. I wanted to give them the same chance to pull their lives together—even though I'm not a therapist. I just help them work through their problems, organize their lives, and make a plan for how they're going to avoid getting sent back."

"That sounds so inspiring. Did your brother have a counselor like that?"

He hesitates before he blurts out, "Yeah. He had me. I was his counselor. I went to visit him once a week and we talked. I helped him figure a few things out. We talked about how we were going to make sure he never got sent back. We talked about Becca and how the situation at home led to him going off the rails. We talked about his old friends who got him into trouble. I supported him and it worked. He got out and he never went back. He has never gotten arrested even once since then. He's never even had a speeding ticket. He's a model husband and father. I'm proud of him."

"Wow," I breathe. "You should be proud of yourself, too."

He shrugs. "Anyway, that's how it started. I started with him and realized I wanted to do this as a job. So I looked into it. I got certified and I applied at the prison. End of story."

"Wow. Color me inspired."

"Your story is really inspiring, too. You struggled through a lot with your head injury. You really pulled it together."

I beam at him. "You're really sweet."

"So are you." He stretches his hand across the table and squeezes mine. His eyes shine.

I smile at him—and in that moment, I realize we aren't acting like brother and sister anymore. This means a lot more. All these touches—all these intimate moments of gazing into each other's eyes—

They might have meant brother and sister before, but they don't anymore. I don't know where we crossed that line, but we did. Maybe we did it right now—right this minute—when he squeezes my hand.

He pulls it back just as fast and we both go on eating, but it's too late.

Chapter 18: Jenn

Marco and I step out of the concourse into the piazza and stop in front of the elevators. We just finished dinner. Now it's time to say good night.

"Are you going to be okay?" I ask.

"Yeah. I'm gonna be fine." He pauses to look into my eyes. "You saved me tonight. I'm really grateful."

"Naw. It was nothing. I just wanted to make sure you were all right. I guess I'll see you tomorrow."

He doesn't answer. He won't stop staring at me.

His eyes give me a fluttery feeling in my stomach. I feel myself getting nervous when he looks at me like that.

I get the feeling again that he isn't looking at me as a friend. We'll never be friends again—or brother and sister or whatever we called it before.

All his comments about meeting his family—they all mean something different now.

Without warning, he takes my hand and pulls me backward onto the rear deck. It's dark outside except for a golden glow coming from the piazza windows.

The darkness swallows us. It's much colder out here in the night sea air.

He walks backward through the door, stops a few feet onto the deck, and cups my cheeks in both hands to kiss me.

I get lost in that kiss. I should tell him to slow down or not kiss me at all, but I don't resist at all—almost as if this was meant to be.

We both felt that everything that happened was for the best. Maybe it happened so he and I could get together.

I kiss him back. That kiss builds in heat and passion with every passing second. It doesn't stop or slow down.

His lips and hands warm my face. His kiss floods my mind with so much peace. I really do love him. I started out loving him as a brother—and I still do.

That's the strangest part in all of this. I know he loves me for who I am. We got to know each other and started to care about each other when neither of us thought there was any possibility that we could ever be together. Being together was the farthest thing from our minds.

Now we're standing in this romantic setting and kissing to the ends of the earth. His kiss feels deep and right and meant to be. It doesn't feel wrong at all. It doesn't feel like I should stop it.

He keeps his hold on my face and doesn't stop kissing me when he moves backward to one of the benches. He sits down and uses his hands around my cheeks to draw me between his knees.

His face sinks below the level of mine, but that only makes his kiss even more intoxicating. I can't stop kissing him. Maybe I'll never be able to stop kissing him ever again.

Is that what this is? Is this meant to be at a deeper level? Is that what our connection is all about—that we were meant to be together for real?

I admire and appreciate everything about him. I admire what he does for work and I admire why he does it. I appreciate so much everything he's done for me and every way he supported me through all of this.

He lets go of my cheeks and wraps his arms around my waist to hug me close while we kiss. His lips don't stop for an instant.

His eyes open and we wind up looking deep into each other's souls while we kiss. He's so much more to me than Donovan was. I never looked into Donovan's soul like this. I can't remember if looking into his soul was even important during our relationship.

He certainly never looked at me like this. He never kissed me so majestically or so tenderly. That's the word that describes Marco. He's beyond tender.

I don't know the moment when it happens, but we both ease back at the same time. Our lips drift apart.

He guides me to sit down next to him on the bench—and then we're kissing again while we sit next to each other. He slips his arm behind my back and pulls me as close as we can get in this position.

It's the most innocent possible position. Nothing can happen as long as we're sitting here like this. Nothing could have happened when we were just standing up with his arms around my waist, either.

I love how he always moves slowly and never does anything to trespass on me. He never pushes me farther than I'm ready to go.

Kissing me is the farthest he has ever gone and he doesn't look like he plans to take it any further. I love that about him. He's always so polite and considerate.

We both finally lean back from that, too. His eyes sparkle inches away from mine as he gives me the last few little pecks. "I guess you aren't my sister after all," he murmurs.

I burst out laughing. "It's probably for the best."

"Yeah," he breathes. "It definitely is. It's worth it to feel you like this."

I gaze deep into his eyes. I can do that with him. His eyes and his heart seem to be made for me to look as deeply into him as I want to.

"When did you know?" I ask. "When did you know it was more?"

"I don't know. Maybe about half an hour ago."

I don't answer. Of course he wasn't thinking that before. I wasn't thinking that at all when he said he loved me as his sister. He thought I really was his sister.

I never thought of him that way, either—not until tonight.

"I don't want to let you go tonight," he murmurs. "I don't ever want to let you go. Stay with me."

I stare into those mesmerizing eyes. "What does that mean?"

He shrugs. "Come upstairs with me. We don't have to do anything. Just stay with me. You're the only company I want on this ship."

"Are you sure about that?"

"Of course. You're the best thing on this ship."

"No, I mean the part about how we don't have to do anything. Are you sure we won't do anything?"

He laughs and his cheeks flush. "We can if you want to."

"Do you want to?"

His expression clears instantly. "Of course I do."

I gasp and pull back. "You do?"

"I want everything with you. I can't imagine anything more perfect than doing everything with you."

I stare at him when I realize exactly what he's saying. He really means everything—like literally everything.

That's what he means about me meeting his family. He might not have been thinking it before, but he's thinking it now.

My mind whirls when I realize all the hidden implications of what he's saying. If I go upstairs with him right now.....

That's the moment when I realize. I want to, too. I wanted this cruise to be a romantic getaway I would remember for the rest of my life.

It won't happen with Donovan, but maybe it could happen with Marco. I feel a lot more romantic toward him than I did toward Donovan.

I actually feel like I could get serious with Marco. I actually feel like I already am—like we're already a couple.

We've already gone through so much together. We've seen each other at our worst and supported each other through all of that. We know each other's deepest secrets.

That's what happened that day on the rear deck when he first told me about Becca. He talked about his family, his past, his troubles, his inner pain....

He told me more than he should have told a total stranger. He confided in me and I was there to support him.

He did the same thing with me when I went through the adoption thing. Who else would I get together with if not him?

He said Donovan was a lucky guy—but Donovan and I had already split up before Marco said that. He thinks anyone who gets with me would be a lucky guy.

He's as caring and protective now as he was when I thought he was my brother. He's all of that and more.

He stands up and takes my hand. "I'll walk you back to your cabin anyway."

We get into the elevator still holding hands. Maybe we'll never do anything more than hold hands and kiss.

I want to. I want everything with him, too. I don't want to just kiss and say good night and see you tomorrow. I want him. I want the whole package.

The elevator opens and we turn toward my cabin. He'll just kiss me good night and walk away. He'll never push it beyond what I'm comfortable with.

I need to take some kind of decisive step. I need to show him that I'm ready, willing, and able to go further with him—all the way if necessary.

He slows down and drags his feet as we get closer to my door. He really doesn't want to leave.

We both stop and turn to face each other outside the door. He caresses his fingers back and forth across my knuckles. "Good night," he murmurs. "I can't wait to see you tomorrow."

"Neither can I—so I'm not going to."

He doesn't understand, so I stick my arm behind me, pass my key card past the reader panel on the door, and the lock clicks.

My gaze rivets on his eyes when I push the door open, walk backward, and lead him by the hand into my cabin. I want him here tonight. I really don't care about anything else.

He's the only man I want. He's the only man who takes the time to make me realize how much I want him. I need him. I need so much more than just to kiss him and hold his hand.

He attacks me the minute the door closes. He circles his arms around my waist and kisses me hard enough to lift me off the floor. I never thought he would let his passion loose like this, but it feels so right.

He stumbles into the wall and catches his weight before he crushes me. He stands there holding me and devouring my mouth as never before. His body simmers with volcanic tension, but he holds it back.

I can't reach any part of him except to run my fingers through his hair. I want so much more of him. I want to tear his clothes off and have my way with him—and for him to have his way with me.

He must think he's going too far. He powers down, sets my feet on the floor, and loosens his arms from around me while we're still kissing like anything.

I don't think he's going far enough. I step back, take his hand, and walk backward into the bedroom. I want him here. I want him in my bed and all over me right this instant.

Chapter 19: Jenn

Marco stares at me in wide-eyed wonder when I lead him into my bedroom. He really didn't think I would go this far.

I don't want to wait for him to take that step. He might not. He might just wait for me to show him what I want.

I ease close to him and push his jacket off his shoulders. He stands there staring deep into my eyes when I pull it off, throw it on the chair, and start loosening his tie.

He lets out a sudden gasp, clamps his eyes shut, and bows his head panting hard in ragged desire. "I need you so bad, baby!" he husks.

"You have me," I whisper and kiss him on the forehead. "You had me at hello."

His eyes open with a very different expression. They smolder with animal ferocity, but he still doesn't move. He stands there seething with barely contained explosive fire while I pull his tie off and start to unbutton his shirt.

The look of raging furious desire burning in those eyes turns me on beyond anything I've ever seen or experienced. His power takes my breath away. I hardly dare to touch him, but I have to.

He rasps through bared teeth when I unbutton his shirt, glide my hands around his waist without taking his shirt off, and bury my face in his chest.

I inhale the satin bliss of his skin under my lips, my hands trailing up his ribs, and his breath straining through his teeth when his hand closes on the back of my neck.

He pulls me up to attack my mouth and we both fall back on the bed locked in each other's arms. I can't stop kissing him. I want to climb on top of him, but he gets there first.

He rolls his weight on top of me and squashes my body under his iron muscular frame. I tear his shirt the rest of the way off, but I can't get to his pants and belt. He won't let me.

His hardness drives me over the edge. He drills his hips into me hard enough to make me whimper. He pushes my legs apart so I can wrap myself around him and feel the waves of pleasure pulsing through me as he rocks harder and faster.

I claw down his back trying to tear his pants off, but he has his own ideas about how to do this.

He crawls down my body to my shirt, gobbles me through the fabric, and catches my nipples with his teeth through my bra cups. I scream as he turns me on. He's already undoing my buttons from the bottom up.

I try to sit up and wind up pushing him all the way up into a sitting position so I can make a grab for his belt.

I miss and my hand comes to rest on his swollen package instead. He gasps and I start to rub him harder.

His eyes lock on me with all his power and he slides his hand between my legs to rub me right where it counts.

I pant harder as he rubs faster. His breath catches as I rub harder. Neither of us looks away for a single instant. He's taking me to the stars too fast. I can't stop it.

He knows exactly where to stimulate me. I whine and sob in aching need and then explode in a blistering orgasm that pours out of me beyond my control. I forget to rub him. He doesn't release—not yet. He takes me there first.

He kisses me harder and pushes me back down on the bed. I collapse in the throes of rapture as his hand glides away and starts working on my shirt buttons again.

He stays up there on his knees and watches me writhe and heave under his hands while he undresses me. His eyes hypnotize me into a sex-fueled trance. I need this. I need him to take me all night.

He pushes my shirt aside to reveal my bra, but he doesn't touch me in any other way. He lets me take the shirt off myself and starts unfastening my pants.

I can only lie here in the haze of the orgasm he just gave me. Why did I think he would just drive by and disappear? Of course he was never going to do it that way.

He tugs my pants down over my hips and pulls my shoes off along with my pants. He leaves my bra and panties on.

I raise my arms above my head and stretch out in front of him. I want him to see me. I want him to be attracted to me and want to take me.

He shifts down the bed and pulls my legs around his waist while he still kneels there between my thighs. He strokes up my legs to my hips, over my belly, and up to my breasts.

He massages them and caresses me through my bra without taking it off. He watches me moan and plead with my eyes for him to do more and more and more.

He doesn't speed up. He doesn't attack. He doesn't do anything but touch me.

He strokes both hands down the curve of my waist to my hips, grips my thighs, and then passes his warm, soft hand down my stomach to the mound under my panties.

He stays there, flattens his fingers against my swollen flesh, and rubs until he makes me sob and gasp and whimper for him.

"You want me to take you, don't you?" he whispers. "You want me to take this as mine. Say you want me to."

"Yes!" I gasp. "I need you so bad, Marco!"

"I'm gonna give it to you, baby," he breathes. "I'm going to make you all mine and never share you with anyone else. No one is ever going to come near you again."

I moan again as the surge of ecstasy hits. He knows exactly how and where to touch me to drive me wild.

I can't go wild when he's looking at me like this. He holds me spellbound while he explores my body with his hands and eyes.

He watches every reaction, every spasm of my facial expression, and hears every moan calling out to him to take me and make me his.

He slides his hands under me and makes me arch my back so he can unclip my bra. His maddening slowness sends me reeling into outer space, but he's only getting started. He leaves me breathless with every touch and graze.

He slides my bra off and the air makes my nipples stand up tight and hard under his hands. I sob and convulse in deepest desire when he touches and plays with them. He already knows I'm his for the taking.

He leaves them reluctantly, migrates down to my panties, and eases them off just as gently.

He has to move out from between my legs so he can push my panties down to my feet and away. Now I'm naked in front of him, but he doesn't go back to touching me—not the way he did before.

He dives between my legs and burrows his ravenous, hungry mouth into me. He blasts me back into screaming ecstasy where I can only thrash and scream on the bed as he spirals me out of my mind.

His fingers explore me, rub my clitoris, and fork my flesh apart to stretch me for his enjoyment. He lifts my thighs to wrap my legs around his neck while he feasts and grips me in mind-blowing climax.

He barely finishes destroying me down to the last particle of my being before he rears off the bed and dives down to kiss me again. He's still wearing his pants and still hard as granite. He doesn't take his pants off.

I want him so bad I can't stand it. I need every inch of his hardness to shatter me and make me whole again.

He drills his hips between my legs and grinds me into another dizzy orgasm. I can't get to him like this. I can't stand how far away he is even when he's lying right here on top of me.

I'm really crying now from this insatiable, unrelenting desire. I can't stand this. I'm really going to burst into tears if he doesn't do it tonight. I can't face that—not after bringing him all the way here.

My dreams come true when he lifts off me, rolls onto his back, and stretches his arms above his head. Now I can see how chiseled and ripped his chest and stomach are.

His stomach muscles contract with the effort of holding back all the energy coursing through him. His shoulders swell when he raises his arms. The line of indentation under his arms runs down to his ribs.

"Take what you want, baby," he whispers. "Take it if you want it. Show me how much you want it."

I have to think about it before I understand what he means. He doesn't come at me again.

He looks as delicious lying there as I thought he would. I want him and now he's giving himself to me.

I rise on my knees—and I realize. I have him in exactly the same position he just had me. I can touch him, kiss him, lick him—drive him to the stars—anything I want.

I want all of that. I want to give him the greatest night of his life so he never forgets this.

I ease over to him, stroke my hands down his chest, over his shoulders, and down to his stomach. I barely graze the bulge in his pants before I scoop my hands up his thighs.

His nostrils flare when I get near his crotch. Then he breathes easier and relaxes when I caress the rest of him.

His body feels amazing. His skin is so soft and warm. He doesn't feel hard or unyielding at all.

I want all of this body in my mouth, in my hands, and between my legs. I want to own this body and for it to own me.

He already owns me. He knows that. He can give me an earth-shattering orgasm whenever he wants. He barely has to try.

Now it's my turn. I stroke him for a long time until I see him fighting for breath. Now he knows how he made me feel.

He never puts his arms down or touches my hands. He exposes himself to my touch. He wants this. He wants me to touch him and feel his body in its purest form.

He keeps no secrets from me. He's mine if I want him. That's the beauty of this. He's already mine.

He lets out a little gasp of agony through his nose when I let my hands travel down to his belt. His prick spasms and strains in his pants. He needs this as much as I do.

He shudders when I slide his zipper down. I love teasing him and listening to him groan the way he made me writhe and sob for him.

He shuts his eyes and turns his head away when I slide his pants down and pull off his shoes. He stretches out in front of me wearing just his shorts.

He wears tight black spandex boxer shorts that leave nothing to the imagination about what's waiting for me inside them, but I'm not ready for that yet.

I stroke up his thighs and over his stomach before I let my hand accidentally fall on his package. I rub and massage him through his shorts until he jolts and thrashes under my hands.

His energy builds to the breaking point, but I ease off every time to let him power down. I keep him trembling like that until I'm ready to pull his shorts down.

His shaft falls into my mouth in all its succulent, throbbing goodness. He whimpers under his breath and his whole body quakes when I start to suck him.

He won't lie still, but he doesn't touch me, either. He doesn't put his hand on the back of my head or squeeze my arms to help him handle the overpowering sensation.

He tries to buck his hips to drive into my mouth. I let him do it for a little while and then ease off so he has to slow down.

I slow way down so he sinks whining and groaning on the bed. I can drive him crazy all night long. Two can play that game.

He doesn't wait that long. He sits up suddenly, pulls me off, and takes hold of my arms to push me down on my back on the bed.

I laugh at him. "What's wrong? You didn't like it?"

He glares at me in fuming desire. "I'll show you what I like."

I grin at him, but my smile vanishes when he rises above me, climbs onto his hands and knees, and crawls up me to ease between my legs.

I squirm into position so I can take all of him. I ache for him. I want him to consume me and devour me with every inch of his body.

His thickness ruptures my mind apart. I need him beyond anything I've ever known.

I try to wrap myself around him, but he stays above me where he can look down at me the way he did before. He watches every sob, every whimper, every grimace, and every rush of ecstasy pouring out of me while he takes me.

I scream out as he picks up speed. He skyrockets me into the stratosphere so much faster than I've ever experienced. I can't take this, but I'm already spiraling out of control too fast.

I seize him in both hands, but I only wind up pulling him in deeper. He slams into me and explodes me out of my mind as all that torrential passion, bliss, and deep connection between us comes to its natural conclusion.

Chapter 20: Marco

I drift awake to feel such a beautiful, immaculate sensation all over me. I've never felt anything like this before.

My mind starts to clear and I realize the feeling is Jenn lying on top of me. She fell asleep there with her magical white thighs still straddling my hips. We're both naked.

She collapsed across me after riding me to another reeling, screaming orgasm. Doing it with her is a dream come true. I start to get hard the minute I wake up—or I might already have been. I can't be sure.

Now she's sound asleep with her face buried in my neck. I have never felt this happy. I'm in her bed. She brought me here to spend one blissful night with her.

Last night was a dream come true, too. I don't want to be anywhere or go anywhere or see anyone. I just want to lie here and feel this.

I've never felt anything so right. Everything that happened led me to this moment. It all worked out for the best.

Now I have to figure out a way to keep her. I have to make her mine. I have to take her home with me and keep her with me always.

That's what I meant last night when I said I didn't want to let her go. I don't want to ever let her go—not ever.

This relationship is some kind of cosmic serendipity. All the forces of creation are bringing us together.

I want to put my arms around her and shower her with love. I want to envelop her and fill her with ecstasy all over again. I just don't want to wake her up.

She stirs pretty soon anyway, groans, and rolls off me. Her thighs leave some of her wetness on my hip. Even that feels like she's christening me with her goodness. Mmmm. She's delicious.

She flops onto her back and rolls away to burrow into the pillows. She better not be trying to go back to sleep.

I scoot in behind her. Now I'm really getting hard. She laughs when she feels me nudging between her thighs from behind.

She pulls away, turns over to face me, and wraps her arms around me so we're facing each other. "Don't you ever stop to sleep?" she mumbles.

"No," I tell her. "Sorry. You're doomed."

She laughs again, sits up, takes my hand, and shoots me a wild smirk. "Come on. Let's take a shower together."

I scramble out of bed. She looks mouth-watering with her hair all messed up like that.

I can't keep my hands off her while she turns on the spray and puts her hand under it to test the water temperature.

She laughs when I grab her breasts and ass, gnaw at her neck, and try to push her forward to bend her over.

She steps into the shower and I climb in with her. She steps under the spray and douses her hair, face, and her whole body. She grins at me with water running all over her face.

I move in to grab her, but she's already dodging me to grab the bottle of body wash. She squirts it into her hand and starts rubbing it over my chest and down my stomach to my stiff shaft.

The suds lubricate her hand and make me mind-bogglingly hot for her. She dives lower, massages my balls until I gasp, and starts soaping me down all over.

She turns me on so much that I can't wait another second. I scoop her up in my arms, kiss her like mad, and pull her thighs around my waist when I push her against the wall.

The shower spray rains down between us, all over our heads, on our faces, and drenches the soap off me so I can plunge into her.

She screams and clutches at me in wild abandon when I start pumping her up the tiles under the shower.

She screams in my ear and her luscious channel welcomes me into the heavenly clouds of glory.

I eventually have to put her down so we can both get cleaned up. I have to stop myself from even looking at her and I definitely don't allow myself to soap her down. That road leads to only one place.

We get out, but we both keep giving each other that look while we dry off, get dressed, brush our hair, and then she lets me use her toothbrush to brush me teeth. I went down on her last night and she went down on me. I guess we share all the same germs now.

We order room service for breakfast. "What do you want to do today?" she asks while we eat.

"You don't really want me to answer that, do you?"

She laughs and blushes. "I mean what else do you want to do other than that?"

"Are we going to spend tonight together, too? Or are we going to go our separate ways and call this a nice memory we can look back on?"

She blushes again. "I think we should spend some more time together outside the bedroom before we make that decision."

I lower my eyes to my plate. "Fine. If we absolutely have to."

She laughs at me. "You said I was your favorite person on the ship. You liked hanging out with me before this."

"Of course I did. I would like hanging out with you even if we never did it."

"Then what are you complaining about?"

"Only that there aren't enough hours in the day to spend with you doing all the things I want to do with you—and I mean *all* the things."

She blushes. "So what are the things you want to do with me—outside the bedroom? What's at the top of your list?"

"Walking around on the deck holding hands and talking about every detail of our lives."

She beams at me. "I like that one. That's at the top of my list, too."

"Great. Then it's settled."

"Do you feel like seeing any shows, acts, plays, musicals, comedy, or movies while we're here?" she asks.

"I didn't see anything on the program that I would consider a must-do—but we can if there's anything you want to see."

"I wouldn't call any of them must-dos, either."

"What about gambling?" I ask.

"I've never gambled."

My head shoots up. "Never?"

"No, never."

"But I met you in the casino. What were you doing there if you weren't gambling?"

"Donovan and I went in there to do an anthropological study of the alien life forms. He went to the bar to get our drinks while I looked around to see if I could understand their language." She laughs and shakes her head at the memory. "That's when I bumped into you."

"You definitely didn't speak my language then."

"What about you? You were gambling that night."

"No, I wasn't. I've never gambled, either. I really don't see the appeal."

"But you were holding a stack of chips in your hand. You were standing next to the table."

"They were Angeline's chips. She wanted to gamble. She bought the chips and then had to go to the bathroom, so I was holding them until she came back. Now I feel like I have something to prove by going to my grave never having gambled even once in my life."

Me, too!" she exclaims. "That is so weird!"

I have to smile at her. "We're cosmic twins."

She laughs and we finish eating so we can go downstairs. We hold hands all the way there and wander around on the deck talking about everything.

She tells me about her sister's family, her cousin Flynn, how he disappeared overseas five years ago, and how she thought Troy Nixon was her cousin when she first came on board the *Electric Emerald*.

She tells me how Donovan got jealous, dumped her, and then started running around with a bunch of other women.

She also tells me her theory that he used her interest in Troy as an excuse to dump her. "I mean, he never acted jealous before—and then after Angeline died, he got all hangdog and contrite and tried to make up with me."

"Maybe you need to have his blood alcohol concentration checked."

She stares off into the distance. "I was thinking drugs, but yeah, you might be right—or maybe it was something else."

"What else could it be? It isn't like he got struck by lightning."

We're just passing through the piazza to head back toward the pools. She stops in the middle of the room to face me. Her eyes take on a new kind of brightness when she looks up into my eyes.

"Maybe it was a different kind of lightning. You know how all these weird coincidences and convergences keep happening to us? Maybe we entered some kind of quantum energy field when we stepped onto this ship. Maybe that's what struck him. Maybe it changed his whole personality so you and I would wind up together."

"That's an interesting theory, but how would you confirm it?"

She doesn't hear me. She glances around her. "Maybe this ship is like an alternate dimension and Donovan and I couldn't be together here. Maybe the ship's energy field broke us apart and put you and me together."

"Does that mean we'll break apart when we leave here?" I cringe. "Angeline isn't out there waiting for me to get back together with her."

She snaps out of her trance and looks up at me. "I didn't mean that. I was just making it up off the top of my head. I didn't mean that at all. I'm sorry. I shouldn't have said that."

"Never mind. Let's go see what's happening on the concourse."

Chapter 21: Marco

Jenn and I head for the concourse when Donovan himself happens to come out of the concourse right then. His eyes harden when he sees us holding hands.

"What do you think you're doing?!" he snaps.

Jenn goes ice cold the minute she sees him. "What I do is none of your business, Donovan. Keep it moving. You aren't welcome in my life."

His eyes dart back and forth between her and me. She doesn't let go of my hand even for an instant. In fact, she tightens her grip on it.

"What are you doing with him?" he demands. "I swear if you're messing around...."

"Kind of like you messed around?" she fires back. "You wouldn't even answer me when I asked how many women you've slept with on this cruise since you dumped me. Huh? What about it? How many women have you slept with on this cruise."

"Well, how many guys have *you* slept with on this cruise, you tramp?"

She snorts at him. "I've only slept with one guy on this cruise." She turns to smile up at me. "He's the best I've ever had." She turns back and sneers at him. "Way better than you, Donovan."

His lips curl back from his teeth. "You son of a bitch!" he roars and lunges for me.

His behavior makes me wary that he might try something like this. He throws a punch, but I dodge it. I duck out of the way and then scoot sideways to push Jenn behind me.

Donovan charges me, but four security guards get to him before he can do anything to me. They grab his arms and wrestle him away against his best efforts to come back at me.

"You filthy bitch!" he rages. "You traitorous slut! You get what you deserve! You betrayed me! You'll pay for this! I swear it!"

His voice fades around the corner as the guards haul him off to the security office. I don't know what to do or if I should do anything.

I turn to Jenn. "Are you okay?" I ask.

She nods fast. "I can't believe he actually tried to attack you! He's out of his mind."

"Kind of like someone else I can think of. Come here. Sit down. You're shaking like a leaf."

I pull her onto one of the benches dotting the piazza. Her hand trembles in mine. She's chalk white and barely looks at me.

"Everything is okay," I tell her. "He's gone. I'm sorry you had to hear that."

"Maybe I shouldn't have baited him like that."

I cup her chin and turn her to face me. "You are not responsible for his actions. There is nothing you could say to him that justifies him turning violent like that. He's been off his rocker since he came on board the ship. This isn't the first time he's gotten in someone's face."

"He tried to push Troy away from me, but Donovan never threw a punch at him."

"He came close," I tell her.

She jolts upright and stares at me. "He did? When? I never saw that."

"No, you weren't there. Donovan cornered Troy in the bar and tried to warn him to back off away from you. Troy tried to reason with him and Donovan chest-bumped him a few times before the guards separated them."

"Oh, my God!" Her hand flies to her head. "I can't believe he's turning into such a psychopath! He always seemed so easy-going and normal before. I don't even recognize him."

"Does he drink much?"

"I..." She breaks off and her shoulders slump. "He has been drinking a lot more since he came on the cruise—but he wasn't drinking the first time he got jealous of me staring at Troy. We just showed up on the boat a few minutes before." She rubs her eyes again. "Something weird is happening."

"It isn't weird. It was meant to be." I squeeze her hand. "Come on. We were having a good time before this happened. We'll walk around and make fun of all the people. Then we can get lunch."

She stands up and follows me in a daze. I know what that feels like. She was the one who took care of me last night. Now it's my turn.

We walk around the concourse for a while before Troy comes up to us. He takes one look at us holding hands and erases it from his awareness.

He nods at me once and turns to Jenn. "Donovan McNulty is being charged with assault, which means he'll be taken off the cruise and extradited back to the States to face criminal charges. I just want you to know. The chopper will be here in two hours to pick him up. You're free to continue with the cruise if you wish—or you can ride back with him. It's up to you."

"Ride back with him?!" she gasps. "Are you crazy? We aren't together! We split up at the beginning of the cruise. I don't want to go anywhere with him!"

He only nods. "I thought you would say that. I had to make the offer, though. You're welcome to stay on the ship for as long as your cruise lasts. Just do me a favor and don't come out on the deck when we load him on the chopper. You can watch from one of the upper deck observation lounges. Just don't let him see you."

"I wasn't planning to."

"Good. Thank you." He nods at me again. "You two have a pleasant rest of your day."

He leaves us alone. I don't feel like eating anything now and I don't plan to take Jenn to any of the activities or entertainment. She blinks at nothing in stunned shock. This is the end. Donovan will be gone in a few hours.

I have to help her. I have to be here for her in all the ways she's been here for me.

I take her over to the elevator and she follows me inside totally oblivious to the outside world. I take her up to the observation lounge—the one overlooking the pools with the chopper pad just beyond that. It's right in the middle of the tennis court.

She'll be able to see everything from here, but Donovan won't be able to see her.

I could just sit here in silence holding her hand. That on its own would be enough, but I want to do more to help bring her back.

I can't stop thinking about last night. She was so good to me when I really needed it.

"So what do you want to get for lunch?" I ask.

She turns in my direction, but she looks straight through me. The lights are on, but no one is home. "Huh?" she asks.

"There's a cake shop up on the fourth deck of the concourse. We could go there and gain ten pounds each."

She bursts out laughing, blushes, and has to cover her mouth. Tears glisten in her eyes when she faces me grinning and blushing like anything. "Yeah. That sounds really good."

"Then we could go to the gym together and work it all off again."

She touches my cheek, leans forward, and kisses me right there in the lounge. She's back. "Or we could drown our sorrows in steak," she suggests.

"As long as it isn't alcohol."

Her expression clears and she looks deep into my eyes. "I know what you mean. I don't think I'll ever see an alcoholic drink the same way again."

I squeeze her hand. "Let's make a pact not to drink again. We can put it in the same category as gambling. It will become one of those things we just never do."

"That's a good idea. It's too bad we both have drunk alcohol before. We won't be able to get to the end of our lives and say we never drank."

"That's all the more reason not to do it. We've both been there and done that. We know what it's like. We don't need to do it again."

"You want to know what's weird—I mean apart from all the other weirdness going on?"

"What's weird?" I ask.

"I never really liked alcohol. I never saw what the big deal was. I mean.....some people seem to treat it like it's really super important. They set aside their entire weekends just to drink and get shitfaced and pass out. Then they wake up the next morning and do it all over again—for the entire weekend. They spend their whole vacations and holidays doing the same thing. I just don't get it. I never found drinking alcohol that fun. I didn't even find it pleasant or appealing or enjoyable. It was just.....there. I don't understand why someone would go out of their way to deliberately shut down the most important parts of their brains."

"Maybe those people hate their lives so much that they can't stand reality," I suggest. "I'm just guessing because I feel the same way you do. I don't see the appeal, but other people seem to think it's like a minimum requirement for any and all social interaction—but maybe they have a reason to want to escape from reality and turn off their brains. Maybe their lives are so terrible that they can't stand it—or they convince themselves that their lives are terrible."

She looks away. "I guess so—but even then, wouldn't you think it would be even more important to keep your brain working—so you could come up with a solution on how to fix it?"

I open my mouth to answer, but right then, we hear the thump of a chopper coming closer. It hasn't been two hours, but maybe the pilot bumped up his timeframe.

Jenn and I get to our feet and approach the lounge windows to watch. We can look right onto the deck as the chopper touches down on the pad.

Some of the security guys come out of the piazza leading Donovan between them. He has his wrists handcuffed behind his back. The security guys lead him by the elbows.

They duck under the rotors and the security guys hand off Donovan to uniformed officers who get down from the chopper to meet him. Some of them help Donovan climb into the chopper.

They unlock his cuffs and re-cuff him with his hands in the front so he can sit back comfortably in the seat. Then they shackle his ankles to the lower part of the seat so he can't move.

Another officer signs off on a tablet one of the security guards hands him. Then all the officers load into the chopper and strap in.

The security guards back away and the chopper lifts off. It floats away toward the eastern horizon getting smaller and smaller. It leaves a heavy silence between me and Jenn.

Donovan is gone. We don't have to worry about him causing trouble for us anymore, but he casts a long shadow. Both he and Angeline do.

It's going to take a while before their ghosts settle down in their graves and stop haunting us.

Chapter 22: Jenn

Marco and I meander out onto the deck near the pools. We don't go near the ship's prow. Neither of us will ever go near that place again.

The bluish, watery glow from the pools makes this part of the deck extra romantic. Marco leans against the railing and rubs my hand while he gazes at me. "We have the whole ship to ourselves. We're all alone here now."

I blush at him. "Not exactly."

"You know what I mean. It's just you and me with no psycho exes running around to ruin our evening. We never have to see them getting drunk with other people or walking around with their arms around their current dates or anything like that."

I murmur, "Yeah," and wind up looking deep into his eyes.

Things have been getting so much more romantic since the chopper took Donovan away. I do know what Marco means. The ship feels different now.

We're both much freer to explore our relationship—much freer mentally. Nothing has changed except that Donovan is gone.

Neither Marco nor I have anyone looking over our shoulders or asking what we're doing or demanding answers about why we're doing it.

We move closer together and our arms slide around each other like we were made this way. Every fiber of my being draws me to him.

We sway in each other's arms kissing, but we drift apart pretty soon and just stand near each other soaking up the environment. Just being together is so peaceful and right.

"So....are we going to spend the night together again?" he finally asks.

"Only if you let me sleep tonight. I can't do another all-nighter like we did last night."

"Let you sleep!" he exclaims. "You were the one keeping me up. I tried more than once to pass out, but you dragged me back and took advantage of me in my weakened state."

I burst out laughing. "You acted willing enough at the time."

"Well, how did you expect me to resist when you threw yourself at me, tied me to the bed, and used me for your pleasure?"

I can't stop laughing. My cheeks flush when I see him smirking at me. "I tied you up, did I? I think you might have been hallucinating."

"I was hallucinating because you drugged me with sex. I couldn't think straight."

"Or maybe you just fantasized about me tying you up."

Now he's the one who bursts into a grin and blushes. "You might be right about that."

"Have you ever done it before?"

He freezes and his eyes drop out of their sockets. "Have I ever done what before?"

"Have you ever gotten tied up in bed—or have you ever tied anyone up in bed?"

"No way! Are you crazy?"

"What's so crazy about it? People do it all the time."

"Crazy people do it all the time! I could never do that!"

"So you were joking just now when you mentioned it?"

"YES!!" He gapes at me. "Why do you ask that?" He gulps. "Have you ever done it before?"

"No, but I don't think it's that unusual. A lot of people do it."

"Do you.....?" He has trouble saying the words. "Do you want to do it?"

I shrug. "I never thought about it. I never thought it was something that interested me, but I would try it if the other person wanted to."

"So.....you don't want me to do it?"

I have to smile when I see him shaking in terror. "I don't want you to do it if you don't want to do it. We won't do it if you're that horrified by it."

His knees sag in relief and he shuts his eyes with a shuddering sigh. "Phew! You had me so worried!"

I laugh at him. "It's no big deal."

"I could never do that!" he exclaims again. "No way!"

"Okay. We won't do it."

"I mean.....you would have to be really twisted to like something like that."

I pat him on the arm. "Okay. We won't."

He barely hears me. "You were the one who said you couldn't understand the appeal of alcohol. How could you get turned on by tying someone down and taking advantage of them—or hitting them with something?! That's insane! I could never do that. I mean—Jesus!"

I can't stop smiling at him. I don't think any of those things is any big deal. It isn't what I'm into, but I understand why other people might get into it.

I also understand why Marco isn't into it. I see both sides, but I don't tell him that. He obviously doesn't want to do it—not that I was planning to do it anyway.

I decide to change the subject. "What did Angeline do for work?"

"She was a curator at an art gallery. She recruited artists to show at the gallery and promoted them to big museums to get their names better known." The subject helps calm him down. "She was really big into art—and she was also really big into entertaining and event planning. She planned a lot of events for openings and showings."

"Maybe that's why she drank so much," I suggest. "Aren't art openings and showings overflowing with alcohol?"

He nods. "Yeah. You're right. It's basically one of the job requirements." He turns back to me. "What does Donovan do?"

"He's the general manager of the Roxbury Hotel. It's a high-stress job—but I never noticed him drinking or anything like that. If anything, his job seemed to make him more grounded."

"Maybe that's why he wigged out—because he got out of his element."

I grin at him, thread my fingers through his, and lean in close to him. "What about you? Are you going to become my life coach?"

"Do you need life coaching? It sounds like you have a career you love—and you aren't in prison or in danger of going there. At least I hope you aren't."

I laugh. "I wouldn't tell you if I was."

He uses our joined hands to bend my arm behind my back so he can pull me against him. "Are you a criminal mastermind in disguise? Are you secretly corrupting all your students into a life of crime?"

I turn bright red. "Actually the opposite. I guess our jobs really aren't that different."

"That's good because the way you make me feel is downright criminal."

I laugh again, but he silences me by kissing me. He pulls me against him, leans back on the rail, and his body stiffens when my weight falls on top of him.

I float away into the dreamy pleasure of our bodies moving in perfect harmony with each other. His desire fuels mine. My body hums with so much desire and adrenaline to feel the way he's going to take me when we go back upstairs.

His other hand follows the curve of my waist to my hip and around to my ass. He squeezes me through my thin satin dress.

His fingers migrate closer to my slit from behind. He pulls me toward him in an unmistakably erotic move of starting to pull my legs apart.

His commanding grip ignites so much passion in me. I gasp and then moan when I feel how hard he is.

Just kissing him sends a gush of wetness into my panties. I remember so much from last night. I remember straddling him while he lies on his back and wrapping my legs around him when he's on top of me.

I see that truth written in his eyes when our lips drift apart. We both know we're going to spend the night together. We'll rock in each other's arms and float in a sea of bliss until morning.

"Are you ready to go?" he murmurs. "We can stay down here if you want to."

"We can go. I'm ready."

He takes my hand and we ride up the elevator. He leads the way to the left this time—toward his cabin.

He doesn't turn on the light. The balcony doors stand open to the sea breeze. It blows its gentle breath into the cabin and makes the gauzy curtains billow inward.

The moon glistens on the ocean out there. I couldn't see it before in the light coming from the pool. Now it casts a silver trail across the water next to the boat. The light creates an even more romantic and blissful atmosphere than the pool did.

I step out onto the balcony to look at everything. The wind blows in my hair. I can't remember anything as romantic as this.

I can't remember being this happy before, either. I've only known Marco for a little while, but I feel happier with him than I ever felt with Donovan—or anyone else.

He steps out there with me, slips his arm behind my back, and looks out at the moon's reflection, too. He doesn't break the silence.

We hover in that dreamy other world here the same way we did downstairs. Everything about us being together feels right. It feels like it's been coming for a long time. We just didn't know it.

I lean against him and he hugs me tighter around the shoulders. Spending the night with him means more than sex. It's about the person he is and how much he accepts and admires the person I am.

We would be together even without the sex. I know that now. Sleeping with him is just the tip of the iceberg.

We have so much yet to explore, but it will happen. We'll find out everything about each other and it will all be good. Nothing can stop that now. It's written in the cosmos—in that beautiful starry sky up there.

We straighten up and face each other. It seems ordained in time that we could come together, wrap our arms around each other, and hold each other close and tight.

I never want to let him go. I want to feel his breath on my skin and his mouth crawling down my neck to bury his face in my shoulder.

I want to feel my fingers in his hair and his shoulders crushing me against him like he wants to push me inside his body to make part of him.

What starts as a hug escalates to something so much more. Our bodies burst to life and he picks me up to lift my feet off the floor. He holds me there while he pushes my dress up and pulls my thigh to his hip.

I climb all the way onto him, straddle him, and we kiss while he carries me back inside the cabin. We don't even get that far before the raging passion between us breaks out.

He stops in the middle of the living room mauling my lips, spiraling his tongue around mine, and riding me down on the hard, throbbing bulge in his pants.

I squeal as each thrust spikes me to the stratosphere. He pushes my dress the rest of the way up, yanks his pants open, and pulls my panties aside to lower me on top of his rigid shaft.

I scream into his mouth, but he doesn't let go of me—my body or my lips. He keeps me locked in that overpowerful kiss while he raises and lowers me on his iron, muscular frame.

I scream again and again as the wave breaks. I reel into another mind-blowing orgasm. It's starting. We'll keep going all night until we both collapse in exhaustion and wake up together tomorrow morning.

Chapter 23: Jenn

I step into my cabin, shut the door behind me, and flop on the bed in my bedroom. I have a few hours to kill while Marco goes to get a haircut. I like his hair the way it is, but he insists he doesn't want it to get too long.

We've been seeing each other for a week since Donovan left the ship. Marco and I started seeing each other before that, but Donovan leaving the ship seems to be the marker by which we measure everything else.

That's when Marco and I really started to focus on each other—now that we don't have to worry about anyone else.

I open my laptop planning to check all my social media accounts. I've been off the radar since I came on the cruise. I've been too busy with all the craziness going on.

I check my email first and find a few different messages from my parents checking in on me. My mom tells me to video call her as soon as I get the message. I hope it's nothing serious.

I switch over to video and send the call through. It takes a minute to connect.

The screen switches on and my mom's face appears. "Hi, Mom," I tell her. "I just got your email. Sorry. Things have been busy here."

"Hold on. Just let me put the computer down so you can see all of us."

She sets the computer on what I recognize as the living room coffee table. She turns the computer to include herself and my dad.

I open my mouth to greet my dad—and freeze when the screen swivels to include Donovan, too. He's sitting on the couch in my parents' living room.

"What are you doing there?" I demand.

"Donovan came to see us, darling," my mom replies. "He says you two had a disagreement and he wants our help to smooth things over."

"We didn't have a disagreement!" I snap. "He dumped me for no good reason and then went around sleeping his way through the rest of the passengers!"

"I'm sure we can work it out if we just keep a civil tone," my dad begins.

"Ask him how many women he slept with on the cruise," I blurt out. "Go on and tell them, Donovan. Tell them how many women you slept with after you dumped me for the crime of asking Troy if he was my cousin, Flynn."

Donovan squirms in his seat. He doesn't look so smug now. "It wasn't like that...."

"Just answer the question! I saw you with at least two different women—and then he got himself thrown off the ship because he took a swing at someone. Did he tell you that? Did he tell you the real reason he came home early when I'm still on the boat?"

My dad turns to Donovan. "You never told us that."

Donovan falters. "I didn't think it was relevant—and she slept with someone, too!"

"I got together with someone *after* you dumped me," I interrupt. "Long after you were out there sowing your wild oats. I at least had the decency to wait until our relationship ended."

My mom starts to say, "I don't know about this……"

"He already tried to get back together with me twice on the ship and I turned him down both times," I go on. "Now he's trying to make an end-run on you two so he can manipulate us all again. It's over, Donovan. Get that through your head and don't come around me or my family again."

Both my parents turn to him. "Is that true?" my dad asks. "How many women *did* you sleep with on the cruise?"

Donovan opens and closes his mouth in flustered confusion for a second. Then he throws up his hands. "I don't have to listen to this!"

He shoots off the couch, storms off the camera, and I hear my parents' front door slam.

"I'm sorry, darling," my mom tells me as soon as silence descends. "We had no idea any of this was going on."

"What's this about you getting together with someone else?" my dad asks. "It's a little sudden, isn't it?"

I heave a giant sigh. "It happened fast. I'll admit that, but he's a really great guy. I told you about him. He's the guy who thought I was his sister. We compared my adoption paperwork with his story and found out I couldn't be his sister—but we got to know each other in the process. We've been seeing each other for a couple of weeks now—and before you ask, yes, we got together long after Donovan broke up with me. I want you both to understand that really clearly. He was the one who walked out on me. He got irrationally jealous and paranoid because I wanted to ask someone if he was Flynn. That's the only reason Donovan dumped me. I never did anything with the guy."

"So the guy you thought was Flynn—he isn't the guy you're going out with?"

"No, no. It's a completely different guy. The man I thought was Flynn is Troy Nixon. He's the Chief of Security on board the ship—and he's married with children. There was never anything going on between us—but Donovan actually got aggressive with him more than once and would have started a fight with him if the other security guards hadn't intervened. Donovan was sleeping around all over the place on the ship. He won't even tell how many women he slept with—so you know it was a lot—and then he threw a punch at Marco, called me a tramp and a slut, got himself charged with assault, and got taken off the ship in handcuffs. You can't sit there and tell me you actually want me to get back together with the guy."

"No, of course not, darling," my mom tells me. "That sounds awful."

"So what's Marco like?" my dad asks. "Do I need to get out the shotgun?"

I laugh. "Nothing like that. He's really nice. We started to feel connected to each other when we thought we might be brother and sister. That's how it started. We both felt like we might be—and we both felt like we might love each other like that—like Fate was bringing us back together. His family has been searching for the sister for twenty-five years, so it was like a dream come true when he thought he might have found her. Then that connection just kind of stayed that way after we found out I wasn't. That's how it started."

My parents both stare at me through the screen until I stop talking.

"You look really happy, sweetheart," my dad remarks. "I never saw you this happy when you were with Donovan."

"I am happy—and you're right. I never felt this way about him."

"Congratulations, darling," my mom tells me. "I'm glad you found that."

"Maybe you guys could meet him. He wants me to meet his family even though I'm not their missing daughter. Maybe we could video chat again sometime and you could talk to him. You could interview him, Dad."

My dad laughs. "I think I better."

"I'll talk to you both later, okay? I better go."

We hang up and I recline on my pillows cruising the internet until it's time for me to go meet up with Marco again.

"You look exactly the same," I tell him. "I can't even tell that you got a haircut."

"No way," he counters. "I looked like Shaggy from *Scooby-Doo* before."

I laugh at him. "I had a video call with my parents earlier. They want to meet you so my dad can give you the third degree."

He only nods. "No problem. I'm good at that."

"You are? What does that mean?"

"I don't know why, but I've always made a good impression on girls' parents when their dads want to question me. Every girl or woman whose parents I've ever met really liked me. They approve of me. I don't understand why other guys dread meeting their dates' parents. It always goes well for me."

"Wow. I wonder why."

He slips his arm around me, leans, and kisses me. "Maybe it's my magnetic aura."

"It must be. You won't believe it. Donovan went over to my parents' house and tried to get them to convince me to take him back."

Marco jolts and gasps out loud. "No way!"

"Can you believe it? He told them some combination of half-truths about how I was sleeping around with someone else. He didn't tell them he did it first and he didn't tell them he got thrown off the ship. Who knows what nonsense he told them?"

"What a slimeball," Marco exclaims.

"Remember when I told you he tried to cozy up to me after Angeline's death and get me to take him back? I asked him then how many women he slept with on the cruise. He wouldn't answer me."

"Holy moly!" Marco remarks. "It must have been a lot."

"I told my parents to ask him—and my dad did. Donovan got really uncomfortable and stormed out."

"So do your parents understand now that he isn't the guy for you?"

"Yeah, they get it now—and they congratulated me on going out with you. They said I look much happier than I ever did with Donovan."

Marco stops and turns to face me. He won't stop smiling. "You make me happy, too."

"I guessed based on the giant grin you've been wearing this past week."

He takes my hand and leads me toward the concourse. "So what's today's fun and excitement?"

"No excitement. I just want to have an easy time for the rest of the cruise. Don't let anything happen. That's an order."

He laughs and leads me into one of the more casual restaurants. "How do you want to do this after the cruise ends?" he asks after we sit down.

I freeze in my seat. "What?"

"How do you want to do this after the cruise ends? How do you want to proceed?"

I gape at him for a second. We never talked about after the cruise ends.

"Is something wrong?" he asks. "*Do* you want to proceed after the cruise ends? We don't have to."

"Yes, I want to proceed after the cruise ends! How can you even ask that?"

"Then how do you want to do it?"

"Um......"

He sits back and skewers me with a hard look. "Just tell me if you don't want to. Don't leave me in any doubt about where this might be going."

"I do want to! Stop saying that! You know I want to!"

"You want to what?"

"I don't know! We never talked about it before!"

"That's why we're talking about it now. Do you need to take some time to think about it? I thought you would have thought about it before now. I certainly have been."

"I just....well, what do *you* want to do?"

"If I had my choice, I would say I want us to move in together. We've basically been living together on this cruise. You stay at my place every night and we spend all day together. I want to continue that once we leave the ship. That's what I want, but I understand if you aren't ready for that. I'm prepared to wait as long as it takes."

I blink at him. "You want.....to move in together...."

"Why not? What's the story with you and Donovan? Do you have to do anything or separate anything once you get back to town?"

"We have an apartment together—but it's rented. I can move out anytime I want to. I was actually planning to rent another place from the ship—so I don't have to think about going back there." I can't stop staring at him. "What about you? Where did you live with Angeline?"

"We owned a house together—but I put it on the market the day after she died. Her family will inherit her half and I'll get a payout for my half. I don't want to move back there and I definitely wouldn't want to live there with you."

I gape at him. "You're serious. You really want us to move in together."

"Of course. Isn't that what we're already doing?"

"I guess so."

He flips his menu over so he isn't looking at me so hard. "It sounds like you want to get your own place for a while before we take that step."

"No!" I blurt out. "I want to. I was just surprised. Don't think anything about it. I want to. So....maybe we should get together and look at places we might want to live."

"What's your financial situation? Would you be interested in buying a house with me?"

My jaw drops all over again. "Are you serious?! You want us to buy a house together?"

"It beats renting. At least you're building equity if you buy something. All the money you would have spent on rent goes into your equity. It builds over time instead of just disappearing into the void."

I gulp. He's actually talking about us moving in together—and co-mingling our funds and all of that.

"I think you better think about it first," he tells me. "Then we can decide if we want to rent or buy."

"No!" I stammer. "We can buy something. I have some savings I can put toward a down payment—and I have a good credit score."

"Why don't we get together like you said and we can take a look around town for something that we like? We might not find anything right away. Then we can rent somewhere until we find something we do like."

I nod at nothing.

"I want you to meet my family, too," he goes on. "I told you that, but it's going to be even more important if we live together."

"Yeah," I choke. "I know."

"My family will love you. I'm certain of it."

My head is still spinning while we eat our meal. I don't know what to think. I've never owned a house with anyone. Donovan and I always rented.

We never shared a bank account, either. We divided all our expenses like we were roommates or something—so I guess we were roommates.

Am I really ready to take that step with someone? I want to. It just scares the crap out of me.

I don't want Marco to think I'm not enthusiastic, though. I want him to know I'm as interested in pursuing a future with him as he is with me.

Chapter 24: Marco

J enn sets her laptop on the coffee table in my cabin living room. She's been living here for over a week since Donovan left. I feel like she's been living here all my life.

She smirks at me when she opens her computer. "You might want to strap on your bulletproof vest."

"It won't be like that. I'm sure your parents will like me."

She smiles and then kisses me. "I'm sure they will."

She turns to the screen, navigates to her video chat app, and checks the time. It's the right time when she's supposed to call her parents and introduce me.

She sends the call through and a middle-aged lady answers. "Hi, Mom," Jenn greets her. "This is Marco de Rossi. Marco, this is my mom, Kathy Hayworth."

"It's great to meet you, Ma'am," I tell her. "Your daughter is really something special—but I guess you already knew that."

Kathy beams at me. "We think so, too, sweetie. Just wait a second. Harlen is here somewhere."

She gets up to go do something. Jenn turns to me while her mom is off the screen. "Really smooth," she murmurs.

"I told you I'm an expert at this."

She giggles, and right then, Kathy comes back with a man her age. "Hi, Dad. This is Marco. Marco, this is my dad, Harlen."

"Great to meet you, Sir," I tell him. "I'm unarmed."

My dad laughs. "I don't even own a firearm, son. You're safe for now."

"Phew," I exclaim. "I was worried."

"No, you weren't!" Jenn counters.

"Jenn has been telling us all about your saga to find out if she was your sister," Kathy interjects.

"Yes, Ma'am. We've been searching for my sister Becca ever since she disappeared. This was the first lead any of us has ever found—so I had to find out. I really appreciate your help with this even if it turned out that Jenn isn't Becca. It's really important to my family."

"We're happy to help, son," Harlen tells me. "I hope your family isn't too disappointed."

"They actually don't know about all of this. I didn't want to tell them before I found out for certain."

"That was probably smart," Kathy tells me. "It's a shame we couldn't give you a better result."

"It was a great result because I met Jenn." I put my arm around her shoulders. "It all worked out for the best in the end."

They both beam at me. "You two look really happy together," Harlen tells me. "I'm happy for you."

"Thank you, Sir. Meeting your daughter is one of the best things that has ever happened to me."

"So tell us how it all went down," he goes on. "How did it happen that you were both so convinced that she was your sister."

I go into the whole story of how Becca disappeared and the affect it had on my family. This is the most I've talked about it to anyone, but it somehow feels natural to share it with these people.

I'm going to be seeing a whole lot more of them if things work out between me and Jenn. I don't want her parents thinking I'm keeping anything from them.

They have a right to know how I met their daughter and what made us get interested in each other. I tell them about the whole Gary, Indiana, connection that tipped us both off that Jenn couldn't be Becca.

Then they ask me questions about my work and how I got into it.

It somehow seems effortless and right that I tell them about Wayne going to prison, too. I can't explain why, but I feel the same effortless desire to share all my secrets with these people the way I share them with Jenn.

Wayne's history isn't really a secret I have to keep from anyone—or at least it doesn't feel that way when I'm talking to Jenn's parents.

It just feels like part of the story of who I am. It's part of the Becca story and the story of how I became the person I am now.

Harlen and Kathy listen through the whole thing. They keep making exclamations about different parts of the story.

Then I tell them how I don't think my job is that different from Jenn's. We both help other people navigate a difficult time in their lives so they can start living more fulfilling, more rewarding lives than they started out with.

"That's quite a story, son," Harlen tells me.

"Yes, Sir. I do seem to be going on about myself. I didn't mean to hijack the conversation."

"It's really interesting. I can see why you and Jenn hit it off. I approve."

I laugh. "Thank you, Sir. That means a lot."

"You could come over for dinner after you both get back to town," Kathy tells me. "We would love to meet you in person."

"I'm certain we will. Thank you for the invitation, Ma'am. It would be an honor."

We get off the call. "See?" I tell Jenn. "Piece of cake."

"You really are something else, you know that?" she tells me.

"I told you I'm good with parents. They always like me."

She won't stop staring at me. "I can see why."

I pull my laptop toward me. "Are you ready for your turn?"

"If I have to."

I laugh. "It will be fine. I think you should sit over there while I explain to them why I want to introduce you to them."

"Okay." She goes to sit on the other couch. I get on my video chat app and call my parents. It's a Sunday there, so I know they're home.

They already know about Angeline's suicide—or whatever it was.

The phone rings and my dad answers. "Hello there, son," he tells me.

"Hey, Dad. How's it going? Are you heating up the barbecue?"

He grins. "I was just about to dump the lighter fluid on the coals. It's too bad you aren't here to help me out."

"I'm sure you can handle it on your own. Is Mom there?"

She sits down next to my dad. "I'm right here, sweetheart. How's the cruise going? I hope you aren't still locking yourself in your cabin all day."

"I'm not. That's actually why I'm calling. I started seeing someone. I want you to meet her. Her name is Jenn and she's a really great person."

My dad frowns. "Is that a good idea for you to start seeing someone so soon after Angeline's death? Don't you think you should take some time to get your life together before you leap into anything?"

"That's what I thought, but Jenn and I have a really great connection and I don't want to wait around before I find someone I like—not when I have someone I like right in front of me."

"You might not be thinking clearly," my mom tells me. "You're on the rebound. You want to find someone to take Angeline's place. You should give yourself some time to find out if this person really is who she says she is."

I feel my hackles rise. "She is who she says she is and I'm as ready to get together with someone else as I'm ever going to be. Jenn is not a rebound."

"You should know better than that," my dad counters. "No one is ever ready to jump into a relationship that soon, especially not when the last relationship ended so badly. You should slow down."

"Just listen to me for a second, okay?" I tell them. "When I first saw Jenn, I actually thought she was Becca."

Both my parents jolt to high alert. "What?!" my dad whispers.

"She looks exactly like the renderings we got of Becca as an adult. I knew I had to find out who this woman was, where she came from, and everything about her."

"Is she?" my mom chokes.

"She can't be," my dad corrects. "He wouldn't be going out with her if she was."

"I talked to her and found out she comes from Wichita Falls, too, but she had never been to Florida. She said she spent her whole life in the Midwest."

My mom droops. "Of course it couldn't be her."

"We had a really good conversation and we connected really well then. She left and called her parents. She mentioned me and they dropped it on her out of the clear blue sky that she was adopted. She had a head injury when she was little and lost her memory. No one knew where she came from and the authorities never found her family—so we thought she might be Becca after all."

My dad's voice trembles. "What happened?"

"We started talking and we both felt like we were brother and sister. We both felt like we had known each other all our lives. Then her parents sent her adoption paperwork and it showed that the Police found her in Gary, Indiana—so there's no chance she could be Becca. That's how it started. We had a really strong connection and she supported me as a friend when Angeline died. It developed from there—so you can see that this isn't a rebound or anything like that. It's the real thing and I want you to meet her. I know you're going to love her."

"I don't know, sweetheart," my mom tells me. "I wouldn't feel right about meeting someone you only just met. Wait a little while and see if this turns into something."

"Your mother is right," my dad adds. "This whole thing might fall apart after you come back to town and real life starts to bite. You still have some work to do to separate yourself from Angeline, the house, her family—all of that. Things are more complicated than you realize."

"It will not fall apart after we get back to town," I growl.

"Just think about it, son," my dad tells me. "Give it time and see where it goes."

I heave a defeated sigh. "All right. I will. See you later."

I hang up and bury my face in my hands. That went so much worse than I thought it would. Will I ever be able to introduce Jenn to my family?

It wouldn't have been so bad if she wasn't sitting right there and listening to every single word. Now she knows they don't trust her or our relationship.

The couch sinks next to me when she sits down and puts her hand on my shoulder. "It's all right," she murmurs. "They have every right to suspect it isn't real."

"It is real! Why can't they see that?" I take my hands down, but I can't straighten up. "Everything was going so well."

"We're bound to run into setbacks and obstacles. This is nothing."

"It is something! My family is as important to me as yours is to you! It won't work if they don't accept you."

"They will," she murmurs. "They're the ones who need time. Be patient."

I look down at my hands. "What if they're right? What if I'm still too messed up from Angeline's death? What if I can't make a decision about what's right for me?"

"Then taking some time will be the best way to decide that." She hesitates. "Maybe I should go stay in my own cabin for a while."

"No. I want you to stay here."

She doesn't answer for a second. "You do need to take at least a little while to work this out for yourself." She kisses the side of my head. "Just take some time to think about it. That's what you told me. Now you need to do the same thing. It will happen if it's meant to be."

She kisses me one more time and walks out. I crumple and cover my face again. This is the worst outcome I could have imagined. My family doesn't want to accept her and now she's going back to stay in her own cabin.

I just want to live with her and start working toward our future together. Now I don't even have that.

Chapter 25: Jenn

I wander out to my living room and go out on the balcony. I'm as happy now as I was after I split up with Donovan.

This is the first time in my life when I've felt perfectly content being by myself. I don't need another relationship—with anyone.

It would be great if things worked out between me and Marco, but I don't need that to be happy.

Taking care of myself is more important. I want to build a future with him, but in a way, I can see that his parents are right. He does need to take some time before he jumps into another relationship.

I wouldn't be doing myself or him any favors if I pushed him into something he isn't ready for—or if I let him push me into something he isn't ready for.

I'm probably not ready for it, either. In fact, I know I'm not.

I turn my face into the sunshine. I need to be okay with being alone—or at least not in a relationship. I *am* okay with being alone. This cruise has been really good for me in that way. I don't need a relationship. I can be this happy all by myself.

I'm taking myself on a romantic cruise—just me, myself, and I. I like this. I don't have to meet anyone's expectations or come to any conclusions.

I go back inside and open my laptop on the couch to search for another apartment to rent. Maybe Marco is right and I should buy something.

I've never thought about that before. I never thought I needed to—so maybe it's a good thing that I met him after all even if things don't work out between us.

I find a lot of apartments I like and some I'm really interested in—both for sale and for rent. I bookmark them and then get in touch with a loan officer to find out how much I could borrow if I did want to buy something.

I'm just going over some of the details and ordering a copy of my credit report when I get a call on my video messaging app. All my good feeling evaporates when I see that Donovan is calling me.

I open the message. "Can I help you?" I snap.

"Can't we just talk, baby?" he asks. "That's all I ask."

"Stop calling me that! What is the matter with you? What part of no do you not understand? We are not together and we never will be. Don't you ever call me that again."

"Isn't there any chance we can work it out? I love you. I'll do anything."

I can't even yell at him to try to make him see sense. "No. There is no chance and there is nothing you can do. It's over and we will never get back together. Don't ask again—and don't give me any problems when it comes to moving out of the apartment. Do you understand? You can stay there by yourself if you want to, but I'm moving out. You better cooperate and be polite about it—and you better cooperate with me taking my name off the lease. If you don't cooperate or if you turn this into a big, ugly, hostile confrontation, then that will be all the proof anyone needs that we never should have been in a relationship at all. If you really care about me—if you're really sorry for what you did—then you should understand why I can't get back together with you. You screwed up."

"I know I did," he chokes. "That's exactly what I'm saying."

"Then you should understand that you screwed up badly enough to spoil any chance of us getting back together. Move on and do better next time. Don't keep nagging me about it—and don't you dare try to mess up my life after this. Just let me go and we can part amicably."

He lets out a broken sigh. "All right. You're right. I will. I won't try to fight you."

"And you better leave Marco alone, too. He lives in Wichita Falls, you know. You better leave him alone—and leave his family alone. Don't make yourself into even more of a violent creep than you already are."

He winces. "It isn't like that."

"Then prove it isn't like that. All your behavior up until now is pointing to that, so you better get busy proving that you aren't. You're going to start with me and Marco. You're going to start being polite, cooperative, and understanding that you're the one who screwed this up. No one did this to you and no one else can fix it. Just walk away from this relationship and don't keep trying to fix it. Just leave me alone. Take yourself out of my life and let me move on, too. If you can't do that, then that only proves that you never cared about me. You were just using me for your own enjoyment and you threw me away as soon as something threatened that."

"I wasn't! It was never like that."

"Then prove it. I'll be coming back to town next week. I'll come by the apartment the following Saturday. Maybe it will be better if you aren't there at all when I come to get my stuff."

He wilts on the other end of the line. His shoulders slump and he looks down at the tabletop in front of him. "Okay," he husks. "I can do that."

"I better go, Donovan," I tell him. "I have a few things I need to do to get ready to come back to town and go back to work and everything."

He doesn't respond and I hang up. Now we'll see how seriously he takes all of this.

I frankly don't trust him not to pull some other nonsense on me or Marco. Then we'll know what Donovan is really made of. He might be incapable of coming back to reality at all.

I switch back over to the real estate listings. I will definitely need a place to live when I get back to town.

I decide to take Marco's advice and rent something while I decide if I want to buy or until I find out if I even can buy something.

I choose the apartment I want and start filling in the application when someone knocks on the door. I open it and find Marco standing outside.

I haven't seen him in three days. We've been taking a break from each other while we both do some serious thinking—or at least I have been.

I see him with new eyes now. I don't need him the way I thought I did. He makes me happy, but I don't need all the drama and baggage that comes along with going out with him.

"Hi," he begins. "How have you been?"

"I've been good. I was just getting another place lined up for when I go back home." I study him more closely. "How have *you* been?"

"I've been good, too. I've been doing a lot of thinking and I was wondering if you would go out to dinner with me tonight. We can take things slowly. We don't have to start talking about moving in together or buying property together or anything like that. I just don't want to lose what we have. It's true that I need to work a few things out within myself after Angeline's death, but what you and I have is too good to let it slip away. I still want us to continue when we get back to town. We can take it as slow as you want to. We can even call each other acquaintances if you want to. We never have to spend the night together or kiss or hold hands or anything like that. I just want to keep seeing you. I want to keep you in my life in whatever capacity you're comfortable with. Maybe in a year or two when things settle down we can think about taking the next step. What do you say? It's just dinner—nothing else. I promise."

I scrutinize him while he talks. He actually does look good. He doesn't look as deliriously happy as he was when we were going out.

I guess that's the whole point. He was delirious. He was drunk on the high of us being together.

He's much more sober now. He knows exactly what he's saying. He isn't falling head over heels for me and what we might be.

He's serious about this being nothing but dinner. What we had before we started going out—what we had when we thought we were brother and sister—it was so good back then.

Both of us could fall back to that whenever we choose to. We would always have that rock solid foundation between us.

That's what brought us together in the beginning and that's what would get us through if it did work out between us.

He means it when he says he would wait a year or two before we took it further. He really would wait that long to prove to both of us that this is real.

I would wait that long, too. I would have no problem just staying in his life as an acquaintance, going out for the occasional dinner, and following each other's progress until we're both ready.

"Okay," I tell him. "I'll go out to dinner with you."

He bursts into a grin, but it isn't his old delirious grin of wild glee. It's a much more serious, down-to-earth smile. "Great. I'll come by and get you at seven. Will that work?"

I smile back at him. I have a good feeling about this. "Yeah," I tell him. "I'll see you then."

"Great. Bye." He walks off toward the elevator. I shut the door. Wow. That is so not what I was expecting.

He's such a good person. This conversation right here makes me believe that we really could work out. He's that serious. I actually love that about him.

I go back to the computer, fill out the rental application, and send it in. I'm going to need a place to live. I might as well get something I like.

Chapter 26: Marco

I knock on Jenn's door and shuffle my feet while I wait for her to answer. We're going out as friends—or acquaintances. That's all.

I don't have any trouble thinking of her that way. She's so great. I would want to keep her in my life even if there was absolutely no chance that we could ever get together.

She answers the door wearing a nice casual outfit. I'm wearing casual clothes, too. This isn't a date. We're just going out socially together as acquaintances.

I can't help but smile just from seeing her again. Three days is a long time when she's right here on the same boat with me.

"Hi," I murmur.

She bursts into a matching smile and she actually blushes. "Hi. Are you ready to go?"

"Yeah. I'll do my absolute best not to try to hold your hand or anything like that."

She only grins at me. "Don't worry about it if you slip up or something. It's really not that big a deal."

She locks her door behind her and we head off down the hall to the elevator. "So did you get your place?" I ask.

"Yeah. I got a really nice place—and I got a call from Donovan. I warned him not to intervene when I move out of the apartment—and I told him to stay away from you. He sounded defeated—like maybe he finally gets it that he can't keep barging around like cock of the walk getting in everyone's faces."

"Thank you," I exclaim. "I was worried about it."

"He agreed not to be there when I go around to get my stuff out of the apartment. So maybe he's finally pulling his head out of whatever dark place he had it buried."

I laugh. "That was a very diplomatic way of putting it."

She grins at me. "I can be diplomatic if I absolutely have to." She gets serious. "How have you been?"

"I've been good—much better than I thought I would be."

"What have you been up to? I haven't seen you around the ship—although I haven't been going out as much. This is the first time I've really gone out."

"I've been doing the same thing. Mostly I've just been going through each day, doing what I need to do, going to the gym, staying active, taking care of some personal business online, handling the sale of my house—whatever comes up that day. I thought I would be wallowing in depression after things fell apart between us, but I haven't been. I've been living my life. It's actually been really good."

"That's great. I'm glad it worked out for you...." She slips her hand into mine. "And things didn't fall apart between us."

I stop in my tracks and stare down at our joined hands. Then my eyes snap up to meet hers. "Really?"

"Yeah!" She smiles up at me. "Really. We had a few speed bumps and I'm sure we'll have a few more. You have stuff to deal with and so do I. That's just life, but things didn't fall apart between us. All the same feelings are still there—aren't they?"

"Of course," I tell her. "How I feel about you never changed. I don't see how it ever can."

"Then nothing is lost. We just need to adjust a few things and overcome a few hurdles before we move on to the next level."

She tugs my arm to keep me moving toward the elevator. I can't believe we're actually holding hands. She wants us to keep moving. That's more than I ever dared to hope for.

We ride down to the concourse and go to one of the nicer restaurants where we won't be underdressed. I don't care if we get fast food and eat on the deck, but I want to show her a nice time.

We sit down and settle in with our menus. "When do you go back to work?" I ask.

"Summer vacation ends in four weeks. We have a teacher-only week before the kids come back. So I'll gear up for the new year then."

"Oh, right. I forgot you were on the school calendar."

"What about you? Can you come and go as you please?"

"Yeah, I make my own schedule, really. Some of the guys I counsel have odd schedules, so I adjust to fit when they're available."

"How can they have odd schedules? They're in prison."

"They have jobs inside the prison. Some work in the laundry. Some work in the kitchen. Some work on the cleaning or maintenance crew. One of my guys just started working in the library. Some of them work the night shift or the later shift or the early morning shift. Sometimes I go in outside of business hours to meet with one of them—and sometimes one of them has an emergency crisis where they need to call me in the middle of the night or if they need me to go in and help them deal with it."

"Wow. That sounds intense."

"It can be—but it's worth it. Some of these guys have no one else in the world. I'm their only support—so it's important that they know they can call on me when they need me." I try to shrug that away. "I guess I think of each of them like Wayne. I would give any of them the same support I would give my own brother. That's what I'm there for."

She rests her chin in her hand to stare at me across the table while I talk. I don't think I'm doing or saying anything out of the ordinary.

She startles me by taking my hand across the table again. "You're a really special person, you know that?" she tells me.

"I'm just doing my job."

"That's exactly what I mean. You don't think it's special. That's what's special about it."

"I don't understand—but thank you. I'll take it as a compliment and not come to the conclusion that you're calling me, 'special' in that way."

She bursts out laughing. "I wish I had a dollar for every time you called me special."

I feel my cheeks burning. "I didn't mean it in that way."

Her eyes twinkle at me and the waitress comes over just then to take our orders. "Don't you dare order anything from the breakfast menu," I tell Jenn.

She laughs again and we both have to pay attention to place our orders before the waitress leaves us alone.

"Now what do you want to talk about?" she asks.

"I really enjoyed meeting your parents. They seem like really nice people."

"They are." She rubs her forehead. "I still don't seem to be able to think of myself as adopted."

"Then don't. Don't think about it. It doesn't make any difference."

"You're right. It just keeps falling farther and farther away into the past ever since I found out. I mean, what difference did it really make in the final analysis? It didn't change anything. It didn't change me and it didn't change the past. They're still my family. My dad is still talking about bringing a firearm to interview someone I'm going out with."

"He said he doesn't own a firearm."

"But he would. He still thinks he has to interview someone I'm going out with—and I still feel like he *should* interview someone I'm going out with. He's still my dad. That didn't change when I found out about the adoption."

"I guess it's like you said. It doesn't change the past. They still raised you. You spent all that time with them. No one can ever erase that."

"Yeah," she breathes. "Exactly."

"I wouldn't want to find out I'm adopted."

She looks up. "Really?"

"Hell no! I wouldn't want another family. Mine is perfect the way it is."

"Do you still feel that way after all the darkness and haunting from Becca's disappearance? Do you still feel that way even knowing how much it affected everyone—like your brother? Do you ever think it would have been better if it had been different?"

"It would have been better if Becca never disappeared, but I wouldn't want another family. It's the best family in a way because we all went through it together. I wouldn't wish what happened to Wayne on my worst enemy, but in a way that worked out for the best, too, because now I can use his experience to help other people. The men I work with would be totally alone with no one if I wasn't there. I can be there because of Wayne. I can be the person these guys need me to be because we all went through that—so maybe that's for the best, too. Maybe this is all part of some cosmic plan and Becca had to disappear so the rest of us could become the people we are now."

She gazes at me across the table. "That is so inspiring."

"You must feel that way, too. You said you became a teacher because of all the teachers who helped you. I don't think it's so different."

"It's still inspiring. I admire you."

Our food comes and the conversation turns to other subjects. We talk about me selling my house and looking for another one to buy. We leave the restaurant and she takes my hand when we wander out onto the deck.

It's another moonlit night with a silver sheen rippling on the waves behind the boat. Jenn's hair billows back in the breeze.

I ease in close to her. "Is this too close?" I ask.

"You don't have to ask that. It isn't like we broke up or anything."

"Really? I didn't realize we were still together."

She beams at me. "We are."

"Does that mean you're going to spend the night with me tonight?"

"You said we would take it slow and I think it's better if we do."

"I don't mind as long as I can still spend time with you. I meant it when I said we could just go out as acquaintances."

"I know you meant it. That's exactly why I decided to go out with you." She squeezes my hand. "I don't want to lose what we have, either. What we have is really good."

"I'm glad you see it that way. Circumstances worked against us, but everything else seems to be right about this."

She beams up at me when she smiles. "Maybe circumstances had to work against us so we would realize how we felt about each other."

I find myself tumbling into the depths of her eyes. "I really want to kiss you right now, so maybe I should walk you home before things spiral completely out of control."

She laughs and we both head for the elevator.

It's nice to know we can both still talk and laugh about all of this the way we did before.

"So you're sure you want us to still be going out?" I ask on the way upstairs.

"We are still going out."

"So....are we calling me your boyfriend now?"

She giggles and smirks at me. "Is that what you want to be called?"

"No, I want to be called your husband, but I can wait on that."

She looks away, but not before I see her blushing.

She doesn't answer and we continue to her door in silence. "Good night," I tell her. "I had a really nice time tonight. I always have a nice time with you."

"Me, too." She grips my hand. "Thank you for asking me out. I wouldn't have taken that step, but I'm really glad you did."

"So can I take you out again sometime?" I ask. "Could we make it a regular thing—since we're still going out—or going out again—or something?"

She laughs. Her eyes don't stop shining with pleasure over everything I say. "Yeah. We could make it a regular thing."

"Great. I guess I'll say good night, then."

"Aren't you going to kiss me?" she asks.

I do a double-take. "Really?"

She blushes and then rises on her tiptoes to kiss me on the lips. It's a feather-light, tender, innocent kiss, but it means so much.

I find my fingertips migrating to her cheek, but she pulls away, smiles again, and squeezes my hand one last time before she pulls away. "I'll see you later."

She slips inside her cabin and leaves me standing there with my head in the clouds. She kissed me.

We've already slept together more times than I can count. Now she's saying we're going out and calling me her boyfriend.

How can one kiss mean so much? It does, though. It means the world. It means more than I ever dared to hope for.

I can wait for the rest of eternity to get back what we lost. I don't care what it takes. I'm going to prove to her and the rest of the world that this is real. Waiting will only make us stronger.

Chapter 27: Jenn

Marco and I get off the plane in Wichita Falls and head down to the baggage claim. We're taking separate cars to our own places, but we've been sharing the last few days together on the trip back home.

"You have my number, right?" he tells me. "Call me if anything comes up."

"I will."

"When are you getting your stuff from Donovan's house?" he asks.

"Saturday. He said he won't be there, but I'll handle it if he is."

"Are you sure you don't want me to come with you and break his kneecaps?"

I laugh. "That's exactly what I don't want you to do."

"Good, because I don't even know how to break someone's kneecaps."

"I'm sure you could call in some of your ex-con buddies to do it for you if you really wanted someone's kneecaps broken."

"No, I couldn't. All my ex-con buddies are going straight now. The whole point is that they don't go back to a life of crime. I wouldn't ask them to—and I wouldn't break someone's kneecaps anyway, especially not Donovan's. The guy is his own worst enemy. He can break his own kneecaps perfectly well, I'm sure."

I can't stop grinning at him. I love talking to Marco about everything.

We get our suitcases and then pay for parking. He eases close to me and kisses me. "I'll call you tonight, okay?"

"Okay. I love you."

"I love you, too. Take care, okay? Drive safely."

"I will. You, too."

We both turn away toward the parking lot to go get our cars. I take hold of my suitcase, but Marco doesn't move.

"Oh, no!" he gasps.

I turn around. "What's wrong?"

"Those guys!" He glances around in panic. "This is terrible!"

I have to look around in all directions, too, before I see two men coming toward us. They're both tall, broad-shouldered, and they have identical short, buzzed hair and crystal blue eyes.

One is quite a bit older than the other. They look like father and son.

"Who are they?" I ask.

"Rod and Ted Harvey—Angeline's father and brother," he husks. "Oh, shit! They look mad!"

They do look mad. Both men brace their shoulders when they barge up to Marco. "We heard you were coming back to town on this flight," Rod snaps.

"And we also heard you hooked up with another woman on the cruise," Ted adds and shoots me a look on the side. "Is this her?"

"Look, whatever it is you have to say to me, you can say it in private," Marco tells them. "We don't need to air this in public."

"Oh, we need to air it in public," Ted fires back. "The whole world needs to know you killed my sister as sure as if you threw her off the ship yourself."

"It wasn't like that," Marco insists.

Rod turns to me. "Did you know about this? Did you know what he did to my daughter?"

I open my mouth to answer, but he turns on Marco and goes on as if I'm not there. "I hope you're satisfied. My daughter gave you everything and this is how you treat her. What did you do to her? How did you drive her into a watery grave? That's what I want to know."

Marco holds up his hand to reason with both of them. "Listen. The Police investigation determined that her death was....."

"Do you think we give a crap about the Police investigation?!" Ted snaps. "You took my sister on a cruise and she came back in a body bag! You were the only one there who could have done anything to her."

"And don't go giving us that shit about it being suicide," Rod interrupts. "Angeline was never suicidal in her life. She could only suddenly have gotten that way because of you."

Marco opens his mouth, but Ted cuts him off. "Don't think we're going to forget about this. We're going to get the Police to reopen the case and prove what you did. You're going to go down for this. Don't think you're getting away with anything, buster. We won't forget."

The two men storm off back to the parking lot. Marco groans and covers his face again. "Not again!" he rasps. "This is the last thing I need."

I touch his arm. "It will be okay. They probably just don't know about the alcohol abuse. She must have hidden it from them, too."

His head swings up fast and he locks his eyes on me. "I can't do this. I can't do anything with you with this hanging over my head. I'm sorry. I need to work this out on my own."

My heart sinks, but I see in his eyes that he's serious. "Okay," I tell him. "I hope it works out for you."

I grab my suitcase and head out to the parking lot without looking back. It's over for real this time and that's the way it should be. He has his own demons to slay and I have a life.

I find my car, drive to my new apartment, and start to settle in. It's a really nice apartment in the back of the building. The apartment is on the ground floor and opens into a beautiful, secluded garden. This is going to be perfect.

I start planning my new life in this apartment. I don't want to take any of the kitchen utensils or anything like that from Donovan's place.

He sent me one email with the new lease agreement for me to sign so my name is removed and he's the only leaseholder. He plans to stay in the apartment, so I agreed to leave all the kitchen gear for him.

I'll need to get new stuff for my new place, but I'm too excited about that to care. I go shopping and enjoy myself getting all the gadgets, spatulas, expensive frying pans, and everything I've ever wanted.

I take my haul back to the apartment, put everything away, and then go grocery shopping so I can make myself dinner tonight. Donovan and I mostly ate takeout or microwaved meals.

I'm going to change that. I'm going to start cooking for myself and I'm going to enjoy it, by God. This is my apartment, my life, and my health we're talking about.

I make up my mind right then to buy my own house. I don't want to wait. I want to start building a home for myself.

I start my dinner cooking and get on the internet to look at some of the real estate listings I bookmarked.

They're all for apartments. I don't want that. I want a real house with a nice kitchen, a yard, and it has to be beautiful. It has to be a real home.

I go back and forth between the kitchen and the computer. I'm going to do this. I'm going to make my life as great as it can be. I'm not going to wait around for anyone to do it for me or make me feel complete.

I un-bookmark all the apartments and start looking at houses. I find five that might work, but none of them really speaks to me. I bookmark them and decide to wait until I hear from the bank before I take the next step.

Chapter 28: Marco

I shut down my computer and get ready to leave my office for the day. The prisoners on the maintenance crew are already turning off the lights for the evening.

I worked late again tonight. I've been doing that a lot since I came back to town. I don't have much of a life outside of work, so I spend a lot more time here.

The guys and the guards call out to me as I pass through the building. They wish me good night and tell me they'll see me tomorrow morning.

I tell them the same thing, get in my car, and drive off, but now I face the same problem as always. Every evening always follows the same routine.

I don't want to go home. I don't even have a home anymore since I sold my house. Now I'm renting an apartment in town while I decide what to do next.

I don't want to buy a real house if I'm going to live there alone. I don't want to buy a cheap, dinky apartment, either. I want a real home, but nowhere feels like home anymore.

I don't know what I'm doing with my life. Work is the only thing that makes sense. I feel like I got run over by a bus—not just from Angeline's death, not just from her family blaming me for killing her, but also from losing Jenn.

I'm the one who ended things, but I still feel the sting of that loss even after almost two months apart. I'm really starting to believe she was the one and now she's gone.

Oh, what the hell am I even saying? She *was* the one. I knew she was the one when we were on the cruise. I told her I wanted to call myself her husband. What else would I mean if not that she was the one?

Now I'm alone and crushed into the dirt even more than if I never met her. This whole cruise experience leaves me battered. I don't know how to come out of it.

I can't go back to that apartment. I almost never go back to it except to sleep.

I drive around for a while and end up going to the park. I spend a lot of time in nature nowadays. That seems to be good for clearing my head.

I get out of the car and walk around in the trees. A bunch of kids play at the pool on the other side of the park. Their shrieks, yells, and screams echo from out of sight.

I slow down and start to relax, now that I'm here alone. I don't have to think or function here.

I walk around the corner and stop in my tracks when I see Jenn bending over a rose bush ahead of me. She's smelling the rose and smiling. God damn, she is so beautiful! She shines with inner radiance that takes my breath away.

She stands up, turns around, and sees me. I don't know what to do, but she walks right up to me. "Hi," she greets me. "How have you been?"

I nod. "I'm getting by. I'm working again, so that's good. How are you? Are you back at school now?"

She smiles at me with all her old genuine understanding. "Yeah. It's all on. The kids are so great. It's everything I remember. Every year is a new adventure. How is work going for you?"

"It's always the same. It feeds the soul, you know? I couldn't live without it."

"That's great. Hey, do you want to go out sometime? I miss you."

I try to look away, but the pure beauty of her soul hypnotizes me. I can't break eye contact. "I don't think I should. I don't want to bring all that negativity back into your life."

"What negativity? You don't have to keep doing penance for Angeline, you know. You weren't responsible for her death no matter what her family thinks. I'm sure they'll come around eventually. You don't have to keep putting your future on hold."

"I know—and you're right, but I'm not ready for that. I want to wait a little longer—maybe a year. I want to make sure I really put it behind me."

Her smile slips ever so slightly. "I won't wait forever, you know. I might meet someone in the next year and you would be left behind stuck in the past. You might want to think about that."

She turns around and my heart plummets into my shoes when she walks off. Now what am I supposed to do?

I blunder back to my car, let my forehead fall onto the steering wheel, and shut my eyes. She's right. I really need to pull it together, but how can I when I can barely function?

I can't function because I don't have her and I can't have her if I can't function. I'm trapped in this cycle of hopeless despair. How could I bring that into her life when she deserves so much better?

I don't want my ability to function to be dependent on being with her. She needs a man who can function on his own without depending on her to make him functional. No one has to explain this to me.

I start the car and drive back to the apartment. I don't even call it my apartment because it isn't. It's a storage unit for a person.

I need to change that. I need to live my life no matter what happens with Jenn or anyone else.

This isn't even about her anymore. It's about me being okay with myself.

She hit it out of the park when she said I need to believe in myself no matter what. I need to believe—I need to know with absolutely no doubt in my deepest heart—that I wasn't responsible for Angeline's death.

It shouldn't matter what anyone else says to me. I should be so solid in my own certainty that they can accuse me of anything they want. It should just roll off me because I know it isn't true.

That's the kind of man Jenn deserves and I'm not that man—not yet. I don't know if I'll ever be good enough for her.

I have to start with this apartment. I start cleaning the place, packing up some of my stuff, and organizing everything in ways I haven't since I moved in here.

I have to move somewhere that is a home. I have to start investing in my own living space as an important part of my life. I can't just keep putting myself in storage. That is unacceptable.

I get on the computer and start looking at the real estate listings. I'm just bookmarking a few that look promising when someone knocks on my door.

I answer it and stiffen when I see Rod Harvey standing there. He's alone, but he looks even more furious than he did at the airport. "Do you got a minute?" he asks in the same short, snapping tone.

"Yes, Sir. I got a minute," I tell him. "Do you want to come in?"

"No, thanks. I'll stay out here if you don't mind."

"What can I do for you?"

He draws in a shaky breath like he needs to do something difficult. "We got a delivery today. It was Angeline's personal effects from the cruise. It looks like....it looks like someone from the ship included a memory stick with a bunch of security camera footage on it. It shows....it shows Angeline screwing around with a bunch of different guys....." He pinches his lips and tears spring to his eyes. "And it shows the footage of her jumping over the side...."

"I'm so sorry, Sir," I murmur. "No one blames themselves for her death more than I do. I just.....I had a really hard time with it...."

He cuts me off with a curt shake of his head. "No! We got the autopsy report with the toxicology results. We had a meeting with the coroner who did the autopsy. We found out about the alcohol....."

He breaks down sobbing right there in front of me. I can't stand it.

I step out of the apartment and grip his shoulder. "I'm sorry, Sir."

"She was out of her mind!" he chokes with tears streaming down his cheeks. His whole body shakes with sobs. "She didn't know what she was doing, did she—with any of it?! She was so tossed she probably didn't even know she was doing it with all those guys.....and then..... she threw herself off the boat...."

He buckles under the weight of despair. Standing this close to him and watching him makes me want to cry, too.

I pull him in and put my arms around him. He grabs me, buries his face in my shoulder, and completely falls apart in racking sobs. Poor guy.

"I'm sorry!" he howls. "I'm so sorry! I never should have blamed you! I didn't know!"

"Okay," I murmur in his ear. "It's okay."

"It's not okay!!" He shoves me back, but he can't stop crying. God, he's hurting so bad! "The coroner said she must have been drinking like that for years—since long before she ever met you! She was gone the whole time you were together, wasn't she?"

"Yeah," I breathe. "That's what I thought."

He grimaces in sobs. "She would have died, wouldn't she? She would have drunk herself to death—or gotten in an accident—or something.....It was only a matter of time!"

"Yeah," I murmur. "The security guy on the ship didn't even think she was trying to kill herself. He says she was just trying to get me to feel bad after she got busted for screwing around."

He keeps trying to wipe the tears off his cheeks, but they just keep coming. "I'm sorry!" he croaks. "I'm so ashamed that we spoke to you like that."

"No!" I murmur. "You don't need to be. I blamed myself. I could have been gentler to her and not told her off as harshly as I did."

He shakes his head. "You had every right to. I would have if I was there. I mean—Jesus! There were more than fifteen guys on that footage."

My eyes fall out of their sockets. "Really? I didn't know it was that many."

He nods fast and then his features spasm again. "I really let her down as a father."

"No, man, not at all. You were a great father. She fell off the wagon all on her own."

"How did this happen?!" he wails. "How did she sink so low?!"

"She was always going to those art openings and gallery showings and everything. She always had to drink at those, remember? It was part of the job."

He crumples up his face sobbing again. I can only stand here and massage his shoulder. I wouldn't wish this on my worst enemy, either.

Angeline's death hits him a lot harder than it hits me. I should feel bad about that, but I don't. Being around someone who is suffering worse than I am brings me back to myself. I'm okay. I'm going to be okay no matter what.

He finally squares his shoulders and glares at me through his tears. "I'm so sorry, son. I don't know if I can ever make it up to you. I can only say I didn't know."

"Forget it. It's over. We both have enough to worry about without holding onto that."

"You're a better man than I am." He coughs and runs his wrist across his nose. "I gotta go. I hope we can meet amicably if we ever see each other again."

"Of course," I tell him. "Always. Tell your family they're in my heart."

His features start to screw up again. He can't speak anymore. He just nods and leaves.

I go back inside and sit down on the couch to stare into space. This changes things—not because he apologized. That isn't it.

He and his family have a much bigger hill to climb than I do.

I'm okay. I'm going to be okay. I can move on after this.

Chapter 29: Jenn

I stir my pasta in the pot and hum to myself when I move over to the cutting board to chop the vegetables for my rigatoni sauce. I really enjoy cooking for myself. It feels like meditation.

I'm just shaking the water off my lettuce for the salad when someone knocks on the door. I open it and come face to face with Marco.

"Are you okay?" I ask.

He takes one step toward me, closes his hands around my face, and kisses me long and deep. He lets all his passion come to the surface with nothing held back.

"You're right. I don't want to wait," he blurts out when he pulls back. His eyes burn with hidden fire. "I want you. I want everything we are—and I want it now. Whatever either of us has to deal with, I want us to go through it together. To hell with everything else. I want to do it now. If you don't want us to move in together right away, then I want us to start going out again. I don't care how long it takes for you to be ready, but I'm ready now. You're the one. You always were the one. I don't want anyone else and I don't want you to want anyone else. I want us to be real—forever."

I gape at him in shock. "You're the one who just told me a few hours ago that you didn't think you should."

"I was wrong. I didn't have my head straight—but I'm okay now. I'm going to be okay—and not because of you. I had to straighten a few things out for myself—but I did that. I'm ready for anything you're ready for. Just tell me what you want to do and I'm there."

I stare up at him. He has never been this determined before—or this articulate. He's never actually come right out and said he wanted all of those things with me.

He did say he wanted to call himself my husband, but he didn't say it as clearly as this.

I have no objection to any of those things—as long as he really is ready.

He is. I see that in his face. He doesn't break eye contact even once. He knows exactly what he's saying and he means it. He means every word.

He said before that he would wait as long as it took. He would do the same thing now. He's deadly serious about all of this.

I ease back and all the tension and uncertainty drains out of me. "Why don't you come inside? We can talk about it."

I step back and wave across the threshold. He steps in and looks around while I go back to the kitchen. "This is a really nice apartment," he remarks.

"I'm really happy with it, but it's only temporary. I decided I want to buy a house—like a real home I can sink my teeth into and make my own."

He looks up. "Really? That sounds awesome."

"I haven't found the right one yet, but I know what I want now. I got pre-approval from the bank for the mortgage, so now I just have to find the house I want to buy."

He sits down on one of the barstools across the counter from me. "So what are you looking for?"

"I'm envisioning something quaint and out of the way—maybe something in the country with big yards and trees and a hammock in the front yard." I chuckle to myself. "It's so strange thinking that way because I've never lived like that before."

"That sounds beautiful."

"It's going to have to be a special place—a place with character. I don't want one of these cookie-cutter modern monstrosities. They're soulless. I want something with a personality all its own—someplace full of the memories and ghosts of families who lived there before me. I want a place that creaks in the middle of the night—someplace that looks like a person looking out at you through the eyes of its windows."

"It sounds like the plot of a movie," he remarks.

I laugh. "A horror movie, you mean."

"No, no, not at all. It just sounds like....like the place has a lot of stories to tell."

I look up and find myself smiling at him. "Yeah. Exactly. That's the problem with these modern places." I look around at the apartment. "This apartment is like that. It's a box. It isn't a home."

He looks away. "I was just thinking the same thing a little while ago. The apartment I've been staying in isn't a home, either."

I stop what I'm doing to look at him while I listen. "Why did you move there? Didn't you plan to buy a house?"

"I did, but I wasn't sure what to buy after we came back from the cruise. I didn't want to buy a full family home if I was going to live there alone. I didn't want to buy a modern apartment, either. I wanted a real place."

A smile spreads over my face. "Yeah! That's how I feel."

"How's school going? Are the kids treating you right?"

"They always do. They love my class—but then again, I only get the kids who want to do music. They're all really enthusiastic and committed. I basically just have to stand back and tell them how great they are."

"I bet they love you."

I blush. "You said it, not me."

He pauses for a second. "What are you making?"

"Rigatoni. Do you want some?"

"It smells delicious. I didn't know you were so into cooking."

"I wasn't. I got onto this whole kick when I moved in here. Donovan stayed in the apartment, so I had to get all new stuff. You could say it inspired me to up my game—but I'm still a fumbling newbie."

"It doesn't smell like you're fumbling at all."

I shoot him a look. I don't want him or anyone else complimenting my cooking.

I serve him a plate and pass it to him across the counter. "I wasn't planning for any dark, handsome stranger to happen upon my door and eat my cooking. Consider that your legal disclaimer before you put it in your mouth."

He bursts into a grin. "Do you really think I'm handsome?"

"Stop it." I take my plate around the counter and sit on the stool next to him. "You can be my crash test dummy."

He laughs and we both start eating. "This is great," he tells me.

"Did Angeline cook?"

"Are you kidding me? I don't think she even knew how to turn on the stove."

I laugh along with him. "I'm sure she had other skills."

He turns on his stool to study me. "Can we talk seriously?"

"About what?"

"About us. About everything I said to you just now about us starting up again, moving in together, and building a future together. We aren't on the cruise. We're back in the real world with real-world problems. You said we could talk about it, so I want to talk about it. What are your thoughts on the subject?"

I turn on my stool, too. "My thoughts on the subject are that we would continue with what we were doing on the boat. We would go out with each other, explore our relationship, and work toward getting more serious. We would agree not to rush into anything too soon before we establish a solid foundation to build on—so we wouldn't move in together right away or anything like that."

"But if you buy a house, then you wouldn't be likely to want to move if we did move in together. I would wind up moving into your house—which means I would want to say something about what the house was." He raises his hand. "Obviously, it would have to meet all your criteria, but if we did this, then it would be our house, not just yours. It would have to be as much my home as yours."

My head shoots up and I find myself staring into his eyes. He would never have said something that to me on the cruise.

He really is a completely different person—but not different. He's just stronger in himself.

He's right. He's going to be okay now and not because of me. He doesn't shy away from challenging me on something like that. He's going to hold me accountable and make sure he's an equal partner in this relationship—if there is a relationship.

I can't hold eye contact with him. I look down at my plate and push my food around. "You're right. We would have to agree on that."

"So here's what I propose. You keep looking for your perfect house and I'll keep looking for my perfect house. If you find anything, you'll tell me and I'll tell you if I find anything. We'll compare notes until we find something we're both thrilled about. Then we can move ahead. I'm sure that will give us plenty of time to develop our relationship and build a solid foundation—since we both want the same thing."

"Okay. I can get on board with that."

"Is there anything you want to add—any modifications you want to make to how we do things or the arrangement we had on the cruise?"

"Not really. It worked out pretty well there, don't you think?"

He nods. "I think so, too. That's why I want to continue it here."

"We should continue with the process of meeting each other's families," I suggest.

"Of course. I completely agree."

"So....." I trail off. "Is there anything else we need to talk about while we're here?"

"Yes. This." He grabs my stool and slides it closer so I'm sitting in front of him nearer than usual. He leans in and kisses me again.

His hands come to rest on my knees and slide up my pants, but he stops at the midpoint of my thighs. He doesn't go any higher.

That one touch brings all my desire back to life. He's going to spend the night here tonight. He doesn't ask and neither do I. We belong together.

My breath catches as a rush of hot liquid fire shoots between my legs. I want to climb onto his lap right now, but I can't do that when we're both fully clothed and sitting here eating dinner together.

Our lips and tongues spiral around each other faster and hotter. His kiss tells me he's thinking about it, too. He wants it. He wants it bad.

I know his body too well not to feel the tension coursing through him. His lips consume me. He won't stop until he conquers his way back into my life and my heart.

We always belonged together. This was always going to happen one way or the other.

It took a long hard road to get here, but it's happening for real now. He won't hold back and neither will I.

Chapter 30: Marco

I get out of the car and open the passenger door for Jenn to get out. She glances toward the house in front of us. It's my parents' house.

She squirms in her tight pencil skirt, pushes it down her legs, and adjusts her blazer sleeves for the thousandth time.

"Don't be so nervous," I tell her. "They know I'm bringing you over to meet them. Everything is going to be fine."

"Maybe this wasn't such a great idea," she croaks.

"We talked about this. I've met your family. Now it's your turn to meet mine."

"I know.....I'm just a bundle of nerves."

"Don't worry about it. You're gonna be great. Come on."

I take her hand and lead her up the driveway to the front door. I keep a hold on her hand when I walk in without knocking.

Wayne's kids run around yelling. I spot my mom and Wayne's wife Torri in the kitchen. I hear my dad and Wayne talking on the deck.

I take Jenn into the kitchen, introduce her to my mom and Torri, and they shake hands and tell Jenn it's nice to meet her.

I take her onto the deck and introduce her to my dad and Wayne. They do the same thing, but it's too smoky out there. I take her back inside just as Torri comes out of the kitchen bringing some plates of food to the table.

"Do you get together with your family all the time?" she asks.

"Every weekend," I tell her. "My dad presiding over the barbecue is a weekend tradition in our family."

She looks around the living room and lowers her voice when Torri leaves to go back to the kitchen. "I'm not getting the whole dark and haunted past vibe here."

I laugh. "We try to tone it down. Like I said, we all try to just move on and live normally."

We have to stop talking about that when my dad and Wayne come in from outside. Torri and my mom bring another load of food to the table and we all stand around talking.

They all make pleasant small talk with Jenn and ask about what it was like on the cruise. They ask about her work and she asks about theirs.

I go into the kitchen to get some drinks out of the fridge for Jenn and myself. When I come back, she excuses herself go to the bathroom and heads down the hall.

I turn to say something to my dad when Wayne interjects, "You're right. She looks exactly like Becca."

My mom presses her hand to her forehead. "I can't do this!"

"You can't do what?" I ask.

"You never should have brought her here!" she moans. "I can't see that face every weekend! This whole relationship is a terrible idea!"

I clamp my mouth shut. "I'm in a relationship with her whether you like it or not. You'll get used to the resemblance. I told you that's how we first started talking to each other. She's the sweetest, nicest person alive. You might even decide to treat her as if she is Becca."

"I couldn't do that!" my mom exclaims. "She's a total stranger."

"She isn't a total stranger to me. She's the woman I love."

"How can you expect us to accept that so soon after you just lost Angeline?" my dad asks. "How can you bring Angeline over here as the woman you love, and the next thing we know, you're bringing over a completely different woman we've never met before?"

"That's why she's here." I try not to snap. "So you can meet her."

"You probably haven't even finished processing Angeline's death," Torri suggests. "You guys were involved right up until the moment of her suicide. How do you know for sure that your relationship didn't contribute to it?"

"It didn't." I really do snap this time. "I know a lot more about it than you do—and it didn't. My relationship with Jenn had nothing to do with it...."

"How do you know?" my dad asks.

"That's my business. I'm not here to air Angeline's dirty laundry."

"You should walk away from this relationship," my mom tells me. "Getting involved with someone who looks like your dead sister...."

"You don't even know if she's dead!" Wayne counters.

I open my mouth to argue back when Jenn walks in just in time to overhear the last part of the conversation.

She comes up behind me. I don't see movement until it's too late. "It looks like I shouldn't be here for this," she remarks.

"No!" I insist. "You have to stay."

"I don't have to do anything." She turns fierce eyes on the other four. "I have no plans to stay where I'm not welcome."

"It isn't like that," my dad tells her. "We just don't see how Marco can get involved with someone so soon after Angeline's death."

"And how he can get involved with someone who looks so much like Becca," my mom adds.

"Does it really matter if I look like Becca?" Jenn asks. "It isn't like he thinks he's involved with his sister."

My mom throws up her hands and turns sideways. "I can't do this! I can't even look at you."

"Just think about it, son," my dad insists.

"I already have thought about it!" I fire back. "How can you be so rude as to talk about this right in front of her? You should all be ashamed of yourselves."

"You're dishonoring Angeline by doing this," Torri tells me. "I'm surprised her family is letting you get away with this."

"You stay out of this!" I spit. "This has nothing to do with you!"

"Take it easy, man," Wayne tells me. "No one is telling you not to get involved with her."

"All of you are telling me that! All of you are telling me to walk away from this relationship."

"You know what? You're right." Jenn turns away. "I don't need this. You all work it out between yourselves."

She walks out of the house. She doesn't even try to soften the blow when she slams the door.

"Are you happy now?!" I rage at everyone. "Let this be the first time in the history of our family when a guest was made to feel so unwelcome that she actually had to leave to get away from your toxic poison."

"We're trying to help you, son," my dad tells me.

"You might consider our feelings for once," my mom adds.

"What the hell do you think I've been doing for the last twenty-five years?!" I roar. "I've been tiptoeing around your feelings every day of my damn life! I've done everything to make you feel better after losing Becca and now you can't even back me up when I want to get just a tiny bit of happiness for myself. What the hell is wrong with you people?"

"You were happy with Angeline," Torri points out. "None of us ever had a problem with her."

"Angeline is dead!! Do you get that?!" I bellow. "Do you really expect me to live alone for the rest of my life?!"

"No, of course not, but....." my mom begins.

"How can you stand there and say I was responsible for her death when her own family admits it wasn't my fault? How can a bunch of strangers support me more than my own family? Tell me that!"

I stalk out of the house simmering with fury, but I have to calm down before I catch up with Jenn.

She's already walking three blocks down the street. This is totally unacceptable. I brought her here so we could start building our future together. My own family had to turn their backs on her and drive her out. Like hell they will.

I run up behind her. "Jenn—wait! Hey, wait!"

She turns around. "You better go straighten out your family, Marco," she tells me in an icy undertone. "It sounds like you guys have some issues to work out. I don't need to get involved in that."

"That doesn't mean anything has to change between us. Come on. Come back to the house and get in the car. I'll drive you home. I'll deal with them later."

She shoots the house a side glance even though it's too far away for her to see. "You go put your house in order before you come near me again."

She turns her back on me and walks off.

I stand there watching her out of sight. She turns another corner. I can't see her anymore. She's right. This is my problem to deal with.

I storm back to the house and push open the door. My parents, Wayne, and Torri all sit around the table eating.

"Sit down, son," my dad tells me.

I remain standing and narrow my eyes at all of them. I'm so mad I can't even raise my voice to yell at them. I can only snarl through gritted teeth to make myself heard.

"I....will never.....sit and eat....at this table.....ever again.....until Jenn is welcome in this house as my partner. You can say whatever you want about her behind her back. Do not EVER let me hear you say anything like that again to her or me."

"You don't have to make it out like that," my dad tells me. "We can talk about this and come to an understanding...."

"We're only going to come to one understanding," I growl. "Angeline cheated on me with over fifteen guys on the cruise and she was wasted out of her mind on alcohol for our entire relationship. She was four times over the legal limit when she jumped off the boat."

Dead silence falls over the table at those words. Maybe now these people will start to understand.

"Jenn is the woman in my life now and that's the way it's going to stay," I go on. "She was the one who supported me and got me through all of that—not you. The very next time I bring her over here, you all better be warm, welcoming, and delighted to see her. I won't come back without her and I won't come back at all if you don't welcome her. Angeline's family doesn't blame me for her death. That should be good enough for everyone. If you don't like it, you can all sit here and have dinner without me. I don't need this and neither does Jenn."

I walk out, get in my car, and drive back to Jenn's apartment. Every word I said to them is true. I won't go back unless they accept her. They have no reasonable cause not to.

I knock on the door. She comes to answer it, but she doesn't open it all the way and she doesn't invite me in.

"I talked to them," I tell her. "I told them what happened on the cruise and I told them I won't go back without you. You won't have to worry about them again. You'll never see them again unless they welcome you."

She doesn't move. She just stands there watching me like she doesn't even recognize me. "I'm not so sure. It sounds like this is your problem to solve, not mine."

"I just solved it. Come on. If something like this happens to one of us, we should face it together. We can't keep turning away from each other every time we hit a bump in the road. You were the one who taught me that."

She stands back. "You can come in, but I'm not ready to go ahead with this until you clear the air with your family."

"I already cleared it. You're with me. That's all anyone needs to know. You'll be welcome if you ever go back there. You never have to hear them talk about you like that and neither will I. I made that clear."

She doesn't answer. She goes back inside the apartment and leaves the door open.

She's cooking in the kitchen again. She's really getting into it, but she doesn't try to talk to me. She doesn't pay any attention to me at all.

I go over there and lean on the counter to talk to her. "I'm sorry you had to hear all of that. You going through it with Angeline was bad enough. We won't go through it here. That's my promise to you. I'll shield you from all of that no matter who it is. Them being my family doesn't make it okay."

She glances up at me for just a minute. "You said that already."

"Hey! I'm serious." I take hold of her arm and try to pull her toward me. "We're together on this. We're in this together."

She resists and pulls away. "I understand you're taking care of it, but I'm not ready to do anything with you tonight. I think you should go. I need to be by myself right now."

I stare at her for a second. We can't be going through this again.

Why can't we be going through it again? I went through it. Now she's doing the same thing.

I wouldn't want to have anything to do with me if I had to hear someone talk about me like that. I can't blame her for getting her feelings hurt.

I raise both hands and back away. "Okay. I can respect that. I'm sorry it happened. I'll do everything in my power to make sure it doesn't happen again. You have my number. Call me if you need anything, okay?"

She nods and I leave. I can only be there for her in whatever way she needs me. I can even leave her alone if she needs it. I love her too much not to.

Chapter 31: Jenn

I walk into the auditorium and get attacked by four huge guys. They grab me, hug me, pick me up off the ground, and jump up and down.

"It's happening, Ms. Hayworth!" Manuel Ortega holds me at arm's length and grins at me while they all laugh. "We're in the finals! We made it to the finals!"

"I know!" I tell him. "When are you on? I can't wait to see you guys perform."

James Walters looks over his shoulder toward the stage. "We have another hour and a half before our spot."

I squeeze his arm. "You guys are going to be great. Just do the same thing you did in practice. That's what got you here."

"You should hear the other bands," Jose Garcia murmurs. "They were amazing—way better than us."

"You can't think like that," I tell him. "You're here to play your best. You earned your spot in the finals. That's something to be proud of, isn't it?"

"Yeah!" Manuel bursts out in excited laughter. "We better get back-stage."

"I'll be watching from the crowd," I tell him. "I'm proud of all of you. You deserve this."

They rush off into the crowd and I make my way inside. The auditorium is already packed.

Most members of the bands scheduled to compete in tonight's RockFest are all adults. Some are professional musicians. These four of my students are the only underage high school kids to make the finals. I couldn't be prouder.

I'm just trying to find my seat when Stu Pendergrass, our school principal, comes up to me out of the crowd. "Did you see the boys?!" he yells in my ear.

"Yeah! They were really happy and excited!"

"They're going to be great. I was planning to give each of them a merit of achievement award at the next school assembly, but don't tell them yet. I want it to be a surprise."

"Wow! Great!" I exclaim. "They'll be thrilled."

He smiles at me and heads off for his own seat. It takes me a long time to elbow my way through the auditorium.

I make it halfway to my seat when I get stopped by another band. They're all huge, burly, bearded, biker types wearing dark sunglasses.

I try to get around them, but their bulk stops me. I glance around for another way to get past.

I freeze when I see Torri and Wayne de Rossi in the crowd. They're talking to some other attendees.

I turn my head to pretend I didn't see them, but not before they both see me. I tap one of the guys on the shoulder, say, "Excuse me," and hustle through their group so I can get to my seat.

I pretend I didn't see Torri and Wayne here. I plan to avoid them for the rest of the evening.

I get through the competition. The boys play exceptionally well and get a standing ovation from the crowd, including me. I'm too over-the-top proud of them to care about anything else.

The organizers hold an intermission between the competition and when they announce the winners. I mingle with Stu and a few other teachers from our school.

We all gush about how well the boys performed and how much recognition we plan to give them when they get back to school.

A bell rings out in the lobby. I'm on my way back to my seat when Torri steps in front of me. "Hi," she begins.

"Uh....hi. I gotta go sit down."

"Those boys.....they're your students, aren't they?" she asks.

"Yes, they are. I'm very proud of them."

"You have a right to be. Listen. I just want to say....I'm really sorry about what happened at the de Rossis' house over the weekend. None of us knew what happened with Angeline on the cruise—and that's still no excuse for the way we talked about you. Marco is right about that—and I want you to know that we all talked after you and he left. We all feel bad for not welcoming you. You're the woman in his life and I promise you will be more than welcome if you ever decide to come back. I understand if you're too angry to come back, but I can only ask you to forgive us and give us another chance. I swear to you on my mother's grave it will never happen again."

I stare at her for a second before I say, "Thanks,"

She nods once, pinches her lips, and hurries back inside the auditorium. I don't know if I can forgive them, but it's nice to know they realize how terribly they acted.

I would never talk about a guest like that—not as long as they were under my roof. I would at least wait until the left the house.

I go back inside the auditorium just as the announcer steps up to the podium. I take my seat. I have much more important things to think about right now.

I white-knuckle it through all the announcements and awards. I can barely sit still in my seat.

Of course the announcer starts with the third-place winner. It's a light-rock girl band with a wispy, Suzanne Vega style lead singer. I didn't think much of that band. This better not turn into a politically correct popularity contest.

Then comes the announcement for the second-place winner. The crowd goes wild when the announcer awards second place to the boys from my music class. I leap to my feet clapping and yelling until my voice and hands ache.

The boys can't stop shaking each other, hugging each other, and James even wipes tears off his cheeks when they receive the award. None of them will stop pumping the announcer's hand.

I barely notice when the bearded biker guys win first place. I don't care. My boys won second. That's incredible. They should all be so proud of themselves.

I can't wait to get out of the theater so I can congratulate them. They're all extremely emotional and ecstatic. They hug me again and again and I hug them back.

We finally part ways. I drive home on cloud nine. This is such a win for me. It shows that my teaching methods are working. These kids got inspired to follow their dreams and it's working.

I can't wait for this week's assembly when Stu honors the boys in front of the whole school. Everyone should know about this achievement and congratulate the boys. They deserve every pat on the back for this.

I go inside my apartment and get ready to change out of my fancy formal dress. We're going to have some work to do come Monday morning. The second-place win puts the boys in the running for the state RockFest competition. They need to prepare for that.

I snicker to myself when I think about how they'll act when they show up to school. They're going to be so much more motivated now. This award is the best thing for them.

I'm just turning off the lights when someone knocks on my door. It's Marco.

His eyes dip to my dress before he pretends I'm not really dressed like this. I wore this dress on one of our fancier dates. He knows how to touch me in this dress.

"Hi," he tells me. "I wonder if you have a minute to talk."

"It's kind of late."

"I know it is. Congratulations, by the way."

"For what?"

"For your students' award tonight. I just talked to Torri. She told me she saw you at RockFest and that she apologized to you for what happened over the weekend."

I look away. "Yeah. She did."

He hesitates a minute and then takes my hand. "Do you think you might be ready to talk to me again—like seriously this time? No more running. No more hiding. No more pushing each other away when things get hard."

I can't look at him. I can only nod before he steps across the threshold.

I fall into his arms and shut my eyes against his jacket. I don't want to be anywhere else. I don't want to run, hide, or push him away anymore.

I can't keep doing this on my own. I can't keep doubting him. I can't keep doubting us. I already know this is right. Why fight it?

Whatever we go through, we have to face it together. He's right about that.

He eases out of my arms, takes my hand, shuts the door with him inside, and leads me over to the couch. He pulls me down to sit next to him, puts his arm around my shoulders, and rests his feet on the coffee table.

"I want to talk to you about something," he tells me.

"Okay," I reply. "What is it?"

He pulls out his phone. "I think I found our house. Take a look and tell me what you think."

He opens his web browser and clicks on one of his bookmarks. It opens to a quaint little country cottage set among sweeping lawns, overhanging trees, and a little creek running past the property line.

I gasp and point at the picture. "I bookmarked this! I saw the same house, but I didn't want to mention it until we straightened things out between us."

"What do you think about going for this house? Is it too soon? We can pass on it and try to find something later."

I look up and our eyes meet. "No," I tell him. "It isn't too soon. We should do it."

"Great. I'll send a message to the realtor that we're interested."

I settle into the crook of his arm while he taps on his phone. The problems slip away into the past—except the ones we can look forward to in the future.

We'll just have to deal with those. We won't be able to run away from each other when that happens.

We'll run toward each other. We'll hold onto each other tighter and lean on each other. That's what this is. We're doing this together come what may.

<u>End of Book 3.</u>

Keep Reading

Paradise Cruises Series: Book 4: Swept Away

Life is returning to normal on board the *Electric Emerald,* but it can never stay that way for long. Barrett Rainey comes on board to attend a business conference and immediately feels drawn to Ariel Dyson, the bartender at his fellow executives' favorite concourse restaurant.

What should have been a routine cruise spirals out of control when another officer in Barrett's company decides she wants him for herself and won't take no for an answer.

Ariel's world comes crashing down around her ears when the unfolding disaster forces Barrett to leave the ship early, but he isn't willing to walk away from what might be his one chance at happiness. He won't let catastrophe stand in his way, but what will happen when he comes face to face with an overwhelming force that not even his undying love can overcome?

You can find it at your favorite book retailer.

Sign Up Once--Get all A.E. Moran's free books including brand new releases

The Paradise Cruise ship *Electric Emerald* is buzzing with the news that Stella Lowell is getting married in two days on board the ship. Stella's family, her fiancé Beau, and Beau's family are all on board and over-the-top excited for the big day.

Too bad Stella isn't over-the-top excited for the big day—or for her fiancé and soon to be husband.

The whole catastrophe blows up when Stella's brother Silas interferes with her talking to a man at the bar. It turns out Silas knows Walker Shockley from their time at school together—and Silas has nothing good to say about Walker.

The disastrous results will be far worse than just a wedding nightmare beyond anyone's worst fears. Nothing is what it seems—and no one is what they seem, either. Life has a way of interfering in the best laid plans. Will the result be the life of Stella's dreams or the worst thing that could ever happen to her?

Sign up at www.authoraemoran.com to read it for free.

About AE Moran

A .E Moran is the contemporary romance pen name for Theo Mann.

I write 70 books per year—and yes, before you ask, all these books are my original creative work. Nothing written under my name is AI-generated or ghostwritten because I write better than AI and any ghostwriter out there.

People don't read fiction for entertainment or to escape from reality. People read fiction to see their humanity reflected in another person's character and story.

This is my promise to you. When you read my books, you'll see your own humanity reflected in the characters and stories. I take this commitment to my readers very seriously. My books are an intimate form of communication between us. I would never disrespect my readers by turning that over to a machine or another writer. This is my bond between me and you as my reader.

I write 20,000 words per day as my daily work output. If anyone with a public platform would like to challenge me to prove this in a controlled environment, feel free to contact me on this website's contact page. How do I do write so much? Find out more on my blog, *Crimes Against Fiction* at www.theomann.com.

I worked as a professional ghostwriter for fifteen years. Now I'm going for the Guinness World Record by writing 700 books over the next ten years and 1400 books over the next twenty years, all originally written by me.

See my website for the full book list. I'm also the author of *Proof for the Existence of God* and the *Crimes Against Fiction* blog.

You can find out more at www.theomann.com or at www.author aemoran.com.

Also by AE Moran (so far)

www.ingramcontent.com/pod-product-compliance
Lightning Source LLC
Chambersburg PA
CBHW070110030726
47506CB00002B/677